Evelyn Cecil

Bibliography of Works on Gardening

Evelyn Cecil

Bibliography of Works on Gardening

ISBN/EAN: 9783337724580

Printed in Europe, USA, Canada, Australia, Japan

Cover: Foto ©Raphael Reischuk / pixelio.de

More available books at **www.hansebooks.com**

BIBLIOGRAPHY

OF

WORKS ON GARDENING

Reprinted from the Second Edition of

"A HISTORY OF GARDENING

IN ENGLAND"

By the Hon. ALICIA AMHERST

LONDON
1897

BIBLIOGRAPHY

OF WORKS ON

ENGLISH GARDENING

————◦◦◦————

PRINTED BOOKS

Arranged Chronologically under the names of Authors or
Translators and under the date of the first edition of their
earliest work;—under the title of the Book and date of the
first edition, when the writers' names are unknown

*An asterisk affixed to any article implies that the book has not
been seen by or for me*

1516 THE GRETE HERBALL. Imprented at London in Southwark
     by me Peter Treveris . . MDXVI, the xx day of June.
     Folio   *
       First Edition. It was described by Ames in his Typographical
       Antiquities; but there is no record of its having been seen by any-
       one since.

The grete herball . . which is translated out yᵉ Frensshe
     into Englysshe . . With the mark of Peter Treveris.
     Folio. Undated   *
       Described by Hazlitt as printed in " 1525-6;" being certainly not
       earlier than 1525, and apparently anterior to the dated issue of
       1526.

The grete herball . . Imprentyd at London in Southwarke
     by me Peter Treueris . . MDXXVI the xxvii day of
     July. Folio
              Several copies are extant.

The grete herball. MDXXVII. 18 April   *
       Such an edition is described by Ames, as printed by Treveris for
       Laurence Andrew.

The grete herball . . Peter Treueris . . MDXXIX, the xvii
     day of Marce. Folio

                                    I *

The grete herball newly corrected.   Londini, in edibus
    Thome Gybson. Anno MDXXXIX.   Folio
The greate Herball .. London, Jhon Kynge, MDLXI.   Folio

1523 [FITZHERBERT'S HUSBANDRY] A newe tracte or treatyse
    moost profytable For All Husbandmen . .
    Imprinted .. by Rycharde Pynson [in or before 1523].
    Small 4to.   *

    In Pinson's edition of Sir Anthony Fitzherbert's Boke of Survey-
    ing, printed in 1523, this book is mentioned as having been already
    published. Its date cannot therefore be later than that year. The
    authorship by Sir Anthony Fitzherbert is considered doubtful, and
    in the B. M. Catalogue it is suggested that John Fitzherbert may
    have been the writer; but it is clear that Pinson and Berthelet
    both regarded the judge as the author. For a full discussion of the
    subject, it will be well to consult the reprint of the Treatise, which
    was edited by W. W. Skeat for the English Dialect Society in 1882,
    and also a paper read by Mr. Ernest Clarke, M.A., F.S.A., before the
    Bibliographical Society in 1896, in which the arguments in favour
    of the authorship of John, Sir Anthony's elder brother, are very
    strong.

—— another edition. Small 4to. in the B. M. supposed to
    have been printed about 1525
—— another edition. Thomas Berthelet, 1534. Small 8vo.
—— another edition, by the same printer in 1548. Small 8vo.
    Various other editions exist.

1525 W. C. [WALTER CARY ?] Here begynnyth a newe mater, the
    whiche sheweth and treateth of ye vertues & proprytes
    of herbes, the whiche is called an Herball. London,
    R. Banckes, 1525. Small 4to.

—— another edition. Robert Redman [1530?]. Small 8vo.

—— A boke of the propreties of Herbes called an herball . .
    Also a generall rule of all maner of Herbes drawen
    out of an auncyent booke of Phisyck by W. C.
    W. Copland for J. Wyght [1552?]. Small 8vo.

    The letters W. C. are supposed by the B. M. cataloguers and by
    the older writers to mean Walter Cary, whose name appears on the
    Farewell to Physicke, printed by Denham in 1583; but others,
    including the writer in the Dict. of Nat. Biogr., take them to mean
    William Copland the printer; and it is to be remembered that they
    occur for the first time in Copland's edition.

—— other editions by Skot and Kytson ; both undated

1527 JEROME OF BRUNSWICK-ANDREW. The vertuose boke of
Distyllacyon of the waters of all maner of Herbes . .
compyled by . . Master Iherom bruynswyke. And
now newly Translate out of Duyche into Englysshe
[by Laurence Andrew]. Imprinted at London . . by
me Laurens Andrewe . . Mcccccxxvii. Folio
The translator (who was also the printer) gives his name in the
Prologue.
(An edition of 1525 is mentioned in Herbert's Ames; but it had
probably no existence.)
There were two issues of the book in 1527, but only the leaves at
beginning and end were reprinted. The body of the book is identical
in each. The first issue is dated the 17 April; the second is dated
the 18 April. They are both in the British Museum.
See also under date 1561.

[1530 ?] MACER-LINACRE. Macer's Herbal practysid by Doctor
Linacro. Translated out of laten into Englysshe . .
R. Wyer, London . (About 1530). 8vo.
—— A newe Herball of Macer . . R. Wyer. (About 1535.)
8vo.

1538 WILLIAM TURNER. Libellus de Re Herbaria novus, in quo
herbarum aliquot nomina greca, Latina & Anglica
habes . . Apud J. Byddellum, Londini, 1538. 4to.
eight leaves
A reprint in facsimile was edited by Mr. B. D. Jackson in 1877,
with a life of Turner. Privately printed.
—— The names of herbes in Greke, Latin, Englishe, Duche
& Frenche wyth the commune names that Herbaries
and Apotecaries use. London, John Day and William
Seres [1548]
—— A new Herball, wherein are conteyned the names of
Herbes in Greke, Latin, Englysh, Duch, Frenche,
and in the Potecaries and Herbaries Latin. London,
S. Mierdman, 1551. Folio
—— The seconde parte of W. Turners herball . . Here unto
is joyned also a booke of the bath of Baeth in
Englande . . Collen, A. Birckman, 1562. Folio
—— The first and seconde partes . . also a Booke of the bath
of Baeth. Collen, A. Birckman, 1568. Folio

1540 [ANDREW BORDE] The boke for to Lerne a man to be wyse in buylding of his howse . . The boke for a good husbande to lerne. Robert Wyer, no date [about 1540]. Small 8vo.

Republished a year or two later by the same printer as part of the Compēdyous Regyment bearing Borde's name.

1557 THOMAS TUSSER. A hundreth good pointes of husbandrie. R. Tottell, London, 1557. In verse

(The copy in the British Museum is presumably unique.) Several varying and augmented editions of the " Hundreth good Pointes " were issued between 1561 and 1571. The first edition of the " Five Hundreth Points " (Tusser's enlargement of the former) came out in 1573.

—— Five hundreth points of good husbandry united to as many of good huswiferie . . R. Tottel, London, 1573 . . 2 parts, small 4to.

Reissued at least twice (in 1576 and 1577) before the appearance of the final and complete edition in 1580.

—— Five hundred pointes of good Husbandrie . . Henrie Denham, London, 1580. Small 4to.

The parent edition of all which followed, and the last which was published by Tusser himself.

The reprints were numerous from that time onwards.

—— Fiue hundred pointes of good husbandrie. The edition of 1580 collated with those of 1573 and 1577 . . with a reprint of "A Hundreth good pointes . . 1557." Edited by W. Payne and Sidney J. Herrtage. Early English Dialect Society, London, 1878. 8vo.

1561 (BRAUNSCHWEIG-HOLLYBUSH) A most excellent and Perfecte Homish Apothecarye, or homely physick booke . . Translated out of the Almaine speche . . by Ihon Hollybush . A. Birckman, Collen, 1561. Folio

It has been alleged that the name of John Hollybush in this book is merely pseudonymous for Miles Coverdale (as it was in the Latin-English New Testament of 1538).

1563 THOMAS HILL. A most briefe and pleasaunt treatyse, teachynge howe to dress, sowe, and set a garden . . T. Marshe, London, 1563. Small 8vo.

Probably the earliest appearance of "the Arte of Gardening." A second edition is unknown.

—— The proffitable Arte of Gardening, now the third tyme
set fourth . . To this annexed, two . . treatises . .
T. Marshe, London, 1568. Small 8vo.

—— The proffitable Arte . . Whereunto is newly added a
treatise of the Arte of graffing and planting of trees.
H. Bynneman, London, 1574. Small 4to.

This edition bears upon its title the statement "now the third
time set forth," just as in the edition of 1568.

Later editions were printed in 1579, 1586, 1593, and 1608, and in
the last two of these a "Treatise on Bees" is included.

The author was probably the same person as Didymus Mountain
who wrote the Gardener's Labyrinth.

DIDYMUS MOUNTAIN [Thomas Hill] The Gardener's
Labyrinth : containing a discourse of the Gardener's
life . . . [completed by Henry Dethick]. H. Bynneman, London, 1577. Small 4to.

Later editions appeared in 1594 and 1608.

1570 MATTHIAS DE L'OBEL Stirpium Adversaria Nova . .
Londini, 1570-71. Folio

Written in collaboration with Petrus Pena, under whose name
it is usually placed.

—— Accessit altera pars . . T. Purfoot, Londini, 1605 . .
3 parts in 1, folio

—— Plantarum seu Stirpium Historia cui adnexum est Adver-
sariorum volumen. Antwerp, Plantin, 1576. Folio

—— Plantarum seu Stirpium Icones. Antwerp. Plantin,
1581. Oblong 4to. (Reprinted in 1591)

1572 LEONARD MASCALL. A Booke of the Arte and maner, howe
to plant and graffe all sortes of trees . . . by one of the
Abbey of Saint Vincent in Fraunce, with an addition
of certaine Dutch practices, set forth and Englished
by L. Mascall. Henrie Denham for John Wight
[1572]. 4to.

Other editions, in 1575, 1580?, 1582, and 1592.

1574 REYNOLDE SCOT. A perfite platforme of a Hoppe Garden . .
London, Henrie Denham, 1574. Small 4to.

Reprinted in 1576 and 1578, "newly corrected and augmented."
Also with other treatises in the "Countryman's Recreation," 1653.

1577 HERESBACH-GOOGE. Foure Bookes of Husbandry, collectèd by M. Conradus Heresbachius . . Newely Englished, and increased, by Barnabe Googe. London, Richard Watkins, 1577. Small 4to.

> Other editions in 1578, 1586, 1614, 1631, and 1658.

MONARDES-FRAMPTON. Joyfull Newes out of the newe founde worlde, wherein is declared the rare and singuler vertues of diuerse . . Hearbes . . Englished by John Frampton . . London, W. Norton, 1577. Small 4to.

> It comprises a description and a woodcut of the Tobacco-plant.
>
> The Spanish author was Nicolas Monardes, frequently styled Dr. Monardus in the editions of the translation.
>
> Reprinted in 1580 and 1596, with some additions.

1578 (DODOENS-LYTE) A Niewe Herball or Historie of Plantes . . set fowrth in the Doutche or Almaigne tongue by that learned D. Rembert Dodoens . . Nowe first translated out of French into English by Henry Lyte . . Antwerpe, 1578. Folio

—— another edition. London, 1586. 4to.

—— corrected and amended. London, 1595. 4to.

—— another edition. London, 1619. Folio

> The English version was made from the French translation executed by Charles de l'Ecluse (C. A. Clusius).
>
> *See* also 1606 : Dodoens-Lyte-Ram.

1579 WILLIAM LANGHAM. The Garden of Health, conteyning the sundry rare and hidden vertues and properties of all kindes of Simples and Plants gathered by long experience and industrie. London, 1579 . . Small 4to.

> Reprinted in 1633.

1586-7 RALPH HOLINSHED. Chronicles of England, Scotland, and Ireland . . London, 1586-87. 3 vols. folio

> This second edition (the first was published in 1577) contains in the description of England (by William Harrison), prefixed to the Chronicle, some references to gardens and orchards in England.

1592 SHORT INSTRUCTIONS very profitable and necessary for all those that delight in Gardening . . . translated out of French into English (𝔟𝔩𝔞𝔠𝔨 𝔩𝔢𝔱𝔱𝔢𝔯). Printed by John Wolfe, London, 1592. Small 4to.

This little book contains 16 woodcuts in 4 gatherings, they are very similar to those in T. Hill's works, some appear to be from the same blocks. The copy belonging to Earl Crewe is probably unique.

1594 SIR HUGH PLATT. The Jewell House of Art and Nature. Conteining diuers rare and profitable Inuentions, together with sundry new experiments in the Art of Husbandry, Distillation, and Moulding . . London, Peter Short, 1594. 4to.

——— Floraes Paradise, beautified and adorned with sundry sorts of delicate fruites and flowers, by the industrious labour of H. P. knight . . London, H. L. for William Leake . . 1608. Small 8vo.

——— the same work, reprinted under the title of The Garden of Eden. 1653. Small 4to.

This edition was brought out, after the author's death, by his kinsman Charles Bellingham, who signs the dedication.

1596 JOHN GERARD or GERARDE. Catalogus Arborum, fruticum ac plantarum tam indigenarum quam exoticarum in horto Gerardi nascentium. Londini, ex off. Roberti Robinson, 1596. Small 8vo.

The copy in the British Museum is probably unique.

——— reprinted in 1876 under the title of "A Catalogue of Plants " . . . with notes. B. D. Jackson . .

——— The Herball, or Generall Historie of Plantes. London, J. Norton, 1597. Folio

——— reprinted with considerable augmentation and improvement by Thomas Johnson in 1633

This immense work of standard character contains 19 preliminary leaves (including the engraved title), 1631 pp. of text, and 46 pp. of tables, etc. It has several hundreds of woodcut illustrations. Most of them appeared in the original edition of 1597, but a large number was added by Johnson in 1633.

1599 DUBRAVIUS—.. A New Booke of good Husbandry .. Written in Latin by Janus Dubravius and translated into English at the speciall request of George Churchey .. London, William White, 1599. Small 4to.

> The translator's name is not known.

GARDNER'S KITCHEN GARDEN. Profitable Instructions for the Manuring, Sowing, and Planting of Kitchen Gardens .. Edw. Allde for Edward White, 1599. Small 4to. *

> This first edition is so described by Lowndes, and is mentioned in Platt's Garden of Eden ; but no copy has been traced.

—— Profitable Instructions for the Manvring, Sowing, and Planting of Kitchin Gardens .. Imprinted at London by Edward Allde for Edward White .. 1603. Small 4to.   *

> This second edition is so described *de visu* in Hazlitt's third Collection of Bibliographical Notes. He calls the author Richard Gardiner ; under which name he seeks to indicate Richard Gardner of Shrewsbury, a dyer and draper, who is described as a public benefactor of that town, in Owen and Blakeway's Shrewsbury.

1600 ESTIENNE AND LIEBAULT-SURFLET.   Maison Rustique or the Covntrie Farme, compiled in the French tongue by Charles Steuens and John Liebault, and translated by Ric. Surflet. E. Bollifant for B. Norton, 1600. Small folio

—— another edition, augmented by Gervase Markham. 1616. Folio

1601 JOHN TAVERNER. Certaine Experiments concerning Fish and Fruit .. Printed for William Ponsonby .. 1601. Small 4to.

1604 N. F. THE FRVITERER'S SECRETS .. London, printed by R.B., solde by Roger Iackson, 1604. Small 4to.

—— reprinted with a different title in 1608 and 1609. *See* below

1606 DODOENS-LYTE-RAM. Rams little Dodeon. A briefe Epitome of the new Herbal or History of Plants .. lately translated into English by Henry Lyte .. abridged by William Ram. London, Simon Stafford, 1606. Small 4to.

See 1578 : Dodoens-Lyte.

1607 DE SERRES-GOFFE. The Perfect Vse of Silk-Wormes and
their benefit . . done out of the French originall of
Olivier de Serres, Lord of Pradel, into English by
Nicholas Goffe . . London, Felix Kyngston, 1607.
Small 4to.

1608-9 N. F. THE HUSBANDMAN'S FRUITFULL ORCHARD, shewing
diuers rare new secrets for the true Ordering of all
sortes of fruite . . London, Roger Iackson, 1609.
Small 4to.

> This work had already appeared in 1608. It is the same book as
> the "Fruiterer's Secrets" of 1604.

1609 W. S. INSTRUCTIONS for the increasing of Mulberie Trees,
and the breeding of Silke-wormes for the making of
Silke in this Kingdome. Whereunto is annexed his
Majesties Letters to the Lords Liefetenants . .
tending to that purpose. London, E. A. for E. Edgar,
1609. 4to.

1612 R. C. AN OLDE THRIFT newly revived . . the manner of
planting, preserving, and husbanding yong Trees . .
London, W. S. for Richard Moore. 1612. 4to.   *
> Described by Hazlitt *de visu* in the Collections and Notes.

1613 ARTHUR STANDISH. New Directions of Experience to the
Commons Complaint . . for the planting of Timber
and Fire-wood . . 1613. 4to.

GERVASE MARKHAM. The English Hvsbandman. The First
Part: contayning the Knowledge of the true Nature
of euery Soyle . . . Together with the Art of Planting,
Grafting, and Gardening . . By G. M. . . London,
T. S. for John Browne, 1613. 4to.

—— The Second Booke of the English Husbandman. Conteyning the ordering of the Kitchen-Garden . .
London, T. S. 1614. 4to.
> The work was reprinted "enlarged by the author" in 3 parts 4to.
> in 1635.   •

—— Maison Rustique. 1616. *See* 1600: Estienne and
Liebault-Surflet

1613 —— The Country Housewifes Garden . . Together with
the Husbandry of Bees . . with diuers new knots for
gardens, by G. M. 1617. 4to.
> The same book was reissued with Lawson's New Orchard in 1618
> and alone in 1620 and 1623.

—— Markhams Farewell to Husbandry ; or, the inriching
of all sorts of barren and sterill grounds . . I. B.
for Roger Jackson, 1620. 4to.

—— The Inrichment of the Weald of Kent . . G. P. for
R. Jackson, 1625. 4to.

—— The Whole Art of Husbandrie, by C. Heresbach,
translated by B. Googe, enlarged by Gervase Markham,
1631. 4to.
> *See* 1577, Heresbach-Googe.

—— A Way to get Wealthe . . 1638-31-38. 4to.
> A compilation of some of Markham's agricultural works, already
> issued separately.

—— The Countrymans Recreation, or the Art of Planting,
Grafting, and Gardening . . London, 1640. 4to.
> Reprinted in 1653 and 1654.

1614 THE MASKE OF FLOWERS . . upon Twelfth Night, 1613 . . at
the marriage of the Earle of Somerset . . N. O. for
R. Wilson, 1614. Small 4to.
> This poetical piece finds a place here as containing, in the *Stage-
> directions*, an admirable description of an Elizabethan garden.

1615 PASSE-WOOD. A garden of Flowers, wherein . . is contained
a . . discription of al the flowers contained in these
foure followinge bookes . . translated out of the
Netherlandish [by E. W. or rather T. Wood ?]. S. de
Roy for Crispin de Passe, Utrecht, 1615. 2 parts,
oblong 4to. 163 plates

1618 WILLIAM LAWSON. A new Orchard and Garden. Or the
best way for planting . . With the Country Housewifes Garden . . B. Alsop for R. Jackson, 1618-17.
2 parts in 1 vol. 4to.

—— second edition. I. H. for Roger Iackson, 1623. 4to.

—— Now the third time corrected and much enlarged . .
Whereunto is newly added the art of propagating
plants (by Simon Harward). I. H. for F. Williams,
1626. 4 parts in 1 vol. small 4to.
> Reissued in 1638 in Markham's Way to get Wealth.

1624 SIR HENRY WOTTON.   The Elements of Architecture . . London, John Bill, 1624.   4to.

1625 FRANCIS BACON (VISCOUNT ST. ALBANS) The Essayes or Covnsels, Civill and Morall, of Francis Lo. Verulam Viscount St. Albans.   Newly enlarged.   4to.
This is apparently the first edition in which the Essay on Gardens was printed.

—— Sylva sylvarum : or a Naturall Historie . . Published after the Author's death.   By William Rawley . . London, 1627.   4to.
The edition of 1676 is called tenth edition.
Rawley was Bacon's chaplain and secretary.

1626 ADAM SPEED.   Adam out of Eden . . London, 1626. 8vo.   *
Watt and Allibone give this date to the first edition, and treat the volume of 1659 as a reprint.   Johnson calls him Adolphus Speed.

—— Adam out of Eden, or an abstract of divers excellent Experiments touching the advancement of Husbandry. London, printed for Henry Brome, 1659.   8vo.

—— The Reformed Husbandman.   1651
This is set down elsewhere as a work by Hartlib.

SIMON HARWARD.   The Art of Propagating plants—printed with the third edition of William Lawson's New Orchard and Garden.   *See* 1618

1629 JOHN PARKINSON.   Paradisi in sole, Paradisus terrestris, or a Garden of all sorts of pleasant flowers . . with a kitchen garden . . and an Orchard.   H. Lownes and R. Young, 1629.   Folio
Reissued in 1635, with an additional letterpress title bearing that date.

—— the second impression, corrected and enlarged.   1656. Folio

—— Theatrum Botanicum.   The Theater of Plants.   Or an Vniversall and compleate Herball . . Tho. Cotes, 1640.   Folio

THOMAS JOHNSON, M.D.   Iter Plantarum investigationis ergo susceptum . . in Agrum Cantianum . . 1629 Julii 13. Ericetum Hamstedianum sive plantarum ibi crescentium observatio . . [Londini, 1629.]   4to.

—— Descriptio Itineris   Plantarum investigationis ergo suscepti in agrum Cantianum anno Dom. 1632, et enumeratio plantarum in Ericeto Hampstediano . . . T. Cotes, 1632.   8vo.

1629 —— Mercurius Botanicus; sive Plantarum gratiâ suscepti Itineris anno MDCXXXIV Descriptio . . T. Cotes, 1634-41. 3 parts 8vo.

—— The Herball . . 1633. Folio. *See* 1597, JOHN GERARD

1639 GABRIEL PLATTES. A Discovery of Infinite Treasure, hidden since the Worlds beginning, whereunto all men . . are . . invited to be sharers with the discoverer, G. P. . . London, Printed for J. E. . 1639. 4to.

—— A Discovery of Subterraneall Treasure, viz. of all manner of Mines and Mineralls . . I. Okes for J. Emery, 1639. 4to.

—— [another edition] Whereunto is added a real experiment whereby every ignorant man . . may try what colour any berry, leaf or wood will give. . . 1679. 4to.

—— other editions

—— The Profitable Intelligencer . . containing many secrets and experiments [with a view to improvement of Agriculture . .]. 1644. 4to.

1640 C. DE SERCY. The Expert Gardener, or a Treatise concerning Gardening and Grafting. London, 1640. 4to. *
Mentioned by Johnson and Watt, but not recorded elsewhere.

(1645 ?) ISAAC DE CAUS. Wilton Garden. [Etchings of the Flower-beds, Fountains, Arbours, etc. of the Earl of Pembroke's Gardens at Wilton.] About 1645. 4to.
Reprinted by Bernard Quaritch, 1895.

—— New and Rare Invention of Water-Works shewing the easiest waies to raise Water higher than the Spring . . Translated into English by Iohn Leak. London, 1659. Folio

1645 SAMUEL HARTLIB. Discourse of Husbandrie used in Brabant and Flanders. London, 1645. 4to.   *
Mentioned in Watt's Bibliotheca.

—— (second edition). 1650. 4to.   *
Mentioned by Weston and Watt.

—— The Third Edition, corrected and enlarged. London, Printed by William Dugard, 1654. 4to. *
Described by Hazlitt *de visu.*

—— Samuel Hartlib his Legacie; or an Enlargement of the Discourse of Husbandry used in Brabant and Flanders . . with Appendix. 1651. 4to.
Other editions in 1652 and 1655.

—— An Essay for advancement of Husbandry-Learning; or Propositions for the errecting Colledge of Husbandry . . London, Printed by Henry Hills, 1651. 4to.

—— The Reformed Husbandman, or a brief treatise of the errors, defects . . of English husbandrie . . 1651. 4to. *
This treatise is elsewhere attributed to Adam Speed. *See* 1626. It appears in Watt under both names.

—— Cornucopia, a miscellaneum of lucriferous and most fructiferous Experiments, observations and discoveries. 1652

—— A Designe for Plentie, by an Vniversall planting of Frvit-Trees. 1652. 4to.
Also issued without a date, and in 1654.

—— A Discoverie for Division or setting out of Land, as to the best forms. Richard Wodenothe, 1653. 4to.

1648 JACOB BOBART. Hortus Medicus Oxoniensis . . Catalogus Plantarum Horti Medici Oxoniensis Latino-Anglicus et Anglico-Latinus. Oxon. 1648. 8vo. 2 parts in 1
The title to the English part is "An English Catalogue of the Trees and Plants in the Physicke Garden of the University of Oxford, with the Latin names added thereunto. Oxford, H. Hall, 1648." The book was reproduced by Simon Paulli at Copenhagen in 1653 in his "Viridaria varia regia et academica."

1649 WALTER BLITH. The English Improver, or a New Survey of Husbandry . . London, J. Wright, 1649. 4to.

—— The English Improver Improved, or the Svrvey of Hvsbandry Svrveyed . . The third Impression . . John Wright, 1652. 4to.

(1650 ?) PETER STENT.   Book of Flowers, Fruits, Beasts, Birds, and Flies . . 4to.   A set of engravings   *

> Ascribed by Hazlitt conjecturally to 1660, but it must have preceded the following. Stent and Simpson were two engravers in London about or before the middle of the seventeenth century.

1650 WILLIAM SIMPSON.   The Second Booke of flowers, fruicts, beastes, birds, and flies exactly drawne, etc.   London, 1650.   4to.

—— another issue.   1661.   4to.

WILLIAM HOW.   Phytologia Britannica, natales exhibens Indigenarum Stirpium sponte emergentium
Londini, 1650.   8vo.

1652 NICHOLAS CULPEPPER.   The English Physitian, or an Astrologico-Physical Discourse of the vulgar Herbs of this Nation.   London, Peter Cole, 1652.   Folio   *

—— another issue.   1652, without publisher's name. 12mo.*

> This is the work popularly known as Culpepper's Herbal. An edition said to be enlarged was printed in 1654, and was the parent of all succeeding issues which have appeared frequently down to the present century.

1653 A BOOK OF FRUITS AND FLOWERS shewing the nature and use of them . . London, 1653

RALPH AUSTEN.   A Treatise of Fruit Trees . . Oxford, 1653. 4to.

—— —— second edition, with the addition of many new experiments.   Oxford, 1657.   4to.

—— —— (another edition, to which are added) Observations upon Sir Francis Bacon's Nat. Hist., also directions for planting wood.   Oxford, 1665.   4to.

—— Observations upon some part of Sir F. Bacon's Naturall History as it concerns fruit trees, fruits, and flowers.   Oxford, 1658.   4to.

> This was the first edition of the "Observations," which were afterwards annexed as a second part to the 1665 edition of the "Treatise."

JOHN BEALE. A Treatise on Fruit Trees shewing their manner of Grafting, Pruning, and Ordering, of Cyder and Perry, of Vineyards in England, etc. Oxford, 1653. 4to.

—— The Hereford Orchards; a pattern for the whole of England. London, 1657. 12mo.

—— General Advertisements concerning Cyder, etc. London, 1677. 4to.

—— Nurseries, Orchards, Profitable Gardens, and Vineyards encouraged (by Anthony Lawrence and John Beal). 1677. 4to.

1656 WILLIAM COLES. The Art of Simpling. An Introduction to the Knowledge and gathering of Plants . . London, J. G. for Nath. Brook, 1656. 12mo.

—— another edition. 1657

—— Adam in Eden, or Nature's Paradise: the History of Plants, Herbs, and Flowers. 1657. Folio

JOHN TRADESCANT. Museum Tradescantianum, or a collection of Rarities preserved at South-Lambeth near London. London, John Grismond, 1656. Small 8vo.

1658 SIR THOMAS BROWNE, M.D. Hydriotaphia, or a Discourse of Sepulchral Urns lately found in Norfolk; together with the Garden of Cyrus, &c. London, 1658

JOHN EVELYN. The French Gardiner . . . Transplanted into English by Philocepos (i.e. J. E.). London, 1658. Small 8vo.

—— Sylva, or a Discourse of Forest-Trees . . To which is annexed Pomona, or an Appendix concerning Fruit-Trees, &c. London, 1664. Folio

—— The English Vineyard Vindicated—see 1666, JOHN ROSE.

—— Kalendarium Hortense; or the Gardener's Almanac, directing what he is to do monthly throughout the year. The second Edition . . London, 1666. 8vo.

The first edition had been issued as portion of the Sylva in 1664.

2

1658 —— A Philosophical Discourse of Earth, relating to the culture and improvement of it for Vegetation . . London, 1676. 8vo.

—— Of Gardens. 4 books. First written in Latin verse by Renatus Rapinus, now made English by J. E. London, 1673. 8vo.

—— The Compleat Gard'ner, &c. . . . by J. de la Quintinye . . made English by John Evelyn . . London, 1693. Folio. 2 vols.

Evelyn's " Directions concerning Melons" forms part of Vol. II. See also 1699 : London and Wise.

—— Acetaria. A Discourse of Sallets. London, 1699 . . 8vo.

1659 ROBERT LOVELL. Παμβοτανολογία, or a Compleat Herbal. Oxford, 1659. 8vo.

—— The second edition, with many additions. Oxford, 1665. 8vo.

Copies of both editions are in the Bodleian.

THOMAS DUCKET. Proceedings concerning the improvement of all manner of land, &c. 1659.

1660 ROBERT SHARROCK. The History of the Propagation and Improvement of Vegetables, by the Concurrence of Art and Nature. Oxford, 1660. 8vo.

—— second edition, much enlarged. Oxford, 1672. 8vo.

—— third edition. London, 1694. 8vo.

JOHN RAY. Catalogus Plantarum circa Cantabrigiam nascentium. Cantab. 1660. 8vo.

—— Appendix ad Catalogum . . Cantab. 1663. 8vo.

These were anonymously published. A second Appendix was printed in 1685.

—— Catalogus Plantarum Angliæ et insularum adjacentium. Lond. 1670. 8vo.

—— Synopsis methodica Stirpium Britannicarum. 1690. 8vo.   *

—— another issue, enlarged. 1696. 8vo.

The Synopsis is an improved edition of the Catalogus of 1670.

—— Catalogus Stirpium in exteris regionibus . . 1673. 8vo.

—— Historia Plantarum generalis. 1686-1688-1704. 3 vols. folio

—— Stirpium Europæarum extra Britanniam nascentium Sylloge. 1694. 8vo.

—— Philosophical Letters . . 1718. 8vo.

> Various other works of this excellent botanist are recorded in Watt's Bibliotheca. His name was originally spelled Wray, but he seems to have dropped the W himself.

1664 JOHN FORSTER. England's Happiness Increased, or a sure and easie remedy against all succeeding Dear Years. By a plantation of the roots called Potatoes. London, 1664. 4to.

LE GENDRE-FORSTER. The Manner of ordering Fruit Trees . . by the Sieur Le Gendre. London, 1664. *

> "Sieur Le Gendre" is a pseudonym for Robert Arnault d'Andilly. The translator was John Forster.

STEPHEN BLAKE. The Complete Gardener's Practice. London, 1664. 4to.

JONATHAN GODDARD, M.D. Observations concerning the texture and similar parts of a Tree.

—— The Fruit Tree's Secrets.

> These treatises were papers read to the Royal Society, and were only printed in Evelyn's Sylva in 1664.

WILLIAM HUGHES. The Complete Vineyard, &c. London, 1665. 4to.

—— The Flower Garden, &c. London, 1671 and 1672. 12mo.

—— The American Physician; or a Treatise of the Roots, Plants, Trees, Shrubs, Fruit, Herbs, etc. growing in the English Plantations . . London, 1672. 12mo.

1665 JOHN REA. Flora, seu de Florum cultura; or a complete Florilege. London, 1665. Folio

—— Flora, Ceres, et Pomona. 1676. Folio

> An enlarged edition of the preceding. John Rea, gentleman, who was resident at Kinlet, near Bewdley, in Worcestershire, in 1676, is sometimes mistaken for John Ray the learned Divine and Naturalist, but the latter was nearly thirty years younger.

Philosophical Transactions, published by the Royal Society, were begun in 1665

> The following are among the contributors to the early volumes (before 1700) of papers on Botanical or Horticultural Subjects— John Beaumont, James Cunningham, John Evelyn, Nehemiah Grew, Hon. Charles Howard, Anthony van Lunwenhock, Martin Lister, Christopher Merret, James Petiver, Robert Plott, John Ray, Richard Richardson, Sir Hans Sloane, John Temple, Ezekiel Yonge.

1666 JOHN ROSE.   The English Vineyard Vindicated . . London, 1666. 8vo.

> With a preface by Philocepos, *i.e.* John Evelyn. It was reissued in a third edition in 1675, as an appendix to Evelyn's French Gardiner.

1667 ABRAHAM COWLEY.   The Garden (a Poem).

> Printed at the end of Poems by Jeremiah Wells, which were published in 1667, in 8vo.

1669 RICHARD RICHARDSON.   De cultu Hortorum, Carmen. London, 1669. 4to.   *

> This title is taken from Johnson's list.† Watt gives the date as 1699.

FRANCIS DUDLEY (fourth Lord North).   Observations and Advices œconomical. 1669. 8vo.

S. B. [SAMUEL BLAGRAVE, or as some say Billingsly.] " The Epitome of Husbandry (a complete plagiary, the first 181 pages being copied from Fitz-Herbert, and the rest from Mascall, &c.)." 1669   *

> This intitulation and note are taken from Johnson.

JOHN WORLIDGE.   Systema Agriculturæ, The Mystery of Husbandry discovered . . To which is added Kalendarium Rusticum . . London, 1669. Folio

> Other editions appeared in 1677, 1681, and 1687.

—— Vinetum Britannicum, or a Treatise of Cider . . London, 1676. 8vo.

> Other editions in 1678 and 1691.

—— Systema Horticulturæ, or the Art of Gardening . . London, 1677. 8vo.

1670 ILIFFE.   The Compleat Vineyard. 1670   *

> This title is given by Johnson. It may be no more than an issue of William Hughes' book. *See* 1665.

LEONARD MEAGER.   The English Gardener, &c. London, 1670. 4to.

—— The Mystery of Husbandry . . to which is added The Countryman's Almanack. 1697. 12mo.

—— The New Art of Gardening; with the Gardener's Almanack. 1697. 12mo.

1672 ROBERT MORISON.   Plantarum Umbelliferarum Distributio. Oxon. 1672. Folio

† See under 1829.

—— Plantarum Historia Universalis Oxoniensis. Pars II. Oxon. 1680

—— Ejusdem Pars III, explevit Jac. Bobartius. Oxon. 1699. Folio

This general work on plants incorporates the earlier " Plantarum Umbelliferarum Distributio," but was itself never completed. Only Parts II and III were written.

—— Icones et descriptiones rariorum Plantarum Siciliæ, Melitæ, Galliæ et Italiæ. Oxon. 1674. 4to.

This is a translation of Paolo Boccone's Manifestum Botanicum.

FRANCIS DROPE. A Short and sure Guid in the practice of raising and ordering Fruit Trees. Oxford, 1672. 8vo.

NEHEMIAH GREW. The Anatomy of Vegetables begun. London, 1672. 8vo.

—— The Anatomy of Plants, with an idea of the Philosophical History of Plants. London, 1682. Folio

1673 RAPINUS-EVELYN. *See* 1658: Evelyn.

1675 CHARLES COTTON. The Planter's Manual, being instructions for the raising, planting, and cultivating all sorts of fruit trees . . London, 1675. 8vo.

1676 MOSES COOK. The manner of raising, ordering, and improving Forrest- [and Fruit-] trees. . . London, 1676. 4to.

1677 ELSHOLT-SHERLEY. Curious Distillatory, or the Art of Distilling Coloured Spirits, Liquors, Oyls, &c. from Vegetables, by J. S. Elsholt, and Englished by Thomas Sherley. London, 1677. 8vo.

1681 T. LANGFORD. Plain and Full Instructions to raise all sorts of Fruit Trees that prosper in England. London, 1681. 8vo.

—— The Practical Planter of Fruit Trees. London, 1681. 8vo.   *

—— second edition, with two chapters of Greens and Greenhouses. 1696. 8vo.   *

The Practical Planter is mentioned by Watt as a distinct work from the Plain and Full Instructions.

1682 SAMUEL GILBERT. The Florists Vade-Mecum . . London, 1682. 12mo.

A second edition appeared in 1683, and a third enlarged in 1702.

1682 JOHN HOUGHTON.   A Collection of Letters for the improvement of Husbandry and Trade.   London, 1682.
4to.

> Issued in numbers in 1681-82.

1683 COMMELIN-G. V. N.   The Belgick or Netherlandish Hes-
perides, that is, the management, ordering and use of
the Lemon and Orange Trees, made English by
G. V. N. (from the Dutch of Commelin).   1683. 8vo.

JOHN REID.   The Scots' Gardener.   Edinburgh, 1683. 4to.

1684 RICHARD HAINES.   Aphorisms upon the new way of improving Cyder, or making Cyder-Royal . . raising and
planting of Apple-trees, &c.   London, 1684.   Folio

1685 [WILLIAM ELLIS.]   The Complete Planter & Ciderist, or
choice Collections and Observations for the propagating all manner of Fruit-Trees . . By a Lover of
Planting.   London, 1685. 8vo.

> The author's name does not appear in the book.

SIR WILLIAM TEMPLE.   Upon the Garden of Epicurus, or
of Gardening in the year 1685

> A treatise on Gardening, especially relating to the Gardens at
> Sheen, written in 1685; published in the Miscellaneous Works of
> Temple, in 1705 and 1720; perhaps also in the edition which had
> appeared in 1689.

THE ART OF PRUNING FRUIT-TREES with an explanation
of some Words which Gardiners make use of . . .
and a Tract of the use of the Fruit of Trees for
preserving us in Health . . . . Translated from the
French original set forth the last year by a Physician .
of Rochelle.   London, Printed for Tho. Basset .
1685. 8vo.

1693 DE LA QUINTINYE-EVELYN.   *See* 1658: Evelyn.

1694 SIR DUDLEY CULLUM.   A new invented Stove, for preserving Plants in the Green House in Winter.   4to.

> Printed in the Philosophical Transactions of 1694.

JOHN PECHEY. The Compleat Herbal of Physical Plants
. . . . London, 1694. 8vo.

1699 LONDON AND WISE. The Compleat Gard'ner [of J. de la
Quintinye, translated by John Evelyn] . . now
compendiously abridged . . with very considerable
improvements. By George London and Henry Wise.
London, 1699. 8vo.

> For the unabridged translation, *see* 1658 : John Evelyn.
> Other editions in 1701, 1704 and 1710.

—— The Retir'd Gardener, from the French of Louis
Liger. London, 1706. 2 vols. 8vo.

—— The Solitary or Carthusian Gardener, from the French
of Francois le Gentil. London, 1706. 2 vols. 8vo.

> The same work, with a different title. Vol. I is from the French
> of Louis Liger. Vol. II from Le Gentil.

FRUIT WALLS improved by inclining them to the Horizon.
1699. 4to.

1700 TIMOTHY NOURSE. Campania Felix, or Discourses of the
benefits and improvements of Husbandry. London,
1700. 8vo.

1702 T. SNOW. Apopiroscopy, or experiments and observations
on several Arts (Building, Agriculture, Gardening,
&c.). London, 1702. 8vo.

1703 LE BLOND—JAMES. The Theory and Practice of Gardening,
translated from the French of A. Le Blond, by John
James. London, 1703. 8vo.

—— other editions. London, 1712 and 1728. 4to.

VAN OOSTEN —. The Dutch Gardener, or the Compleat
Florist . . written in Dutch by Henry Van Oosten,
the Leyden Gardener. And made English. London,
Printed for D. Midwinter and T. Leigh . . . . 1703.
Small 8vo.

—— another edition, 1711   *

1704 SMITH.   The Husbandman's Magazine.   1704   *
    Only mentioned by Johnson.

Dictionarium Rusticum et Urbanicum. A Dictionary of
  all sorts of County Affairs, trading, &c. London,
  1704. 8vo. Anonymous

1706 RICHARD BRADLEY.   Paintings of his succulent plants, with
  written accounts of them.   1706

—— A treatise on Succulent Plants. London, 1710

—— Historia Plantarum succulentarum. London, 1716-27.
  4to.

—— New Improvements of planting and gardening, philosophical and practical. London, 1717. 8vo.
    Several later editions—the 6th, 1731.

—— The Gentleman and Gardener's Kalendar. London,
  1718. 8vo.

—— A Philosophical Account of the Works of Nature.
  London, 1721. 4to.

—— A Survey of Ancient Husbandry and Gardening. London, 1725. 8vo.

—— A general Treatise of Husbandry and Gardening.
  Formerly published monthly, now methodized and
  digested. London, 1726. 2 vols. 8vo.

—— A complete Body of Husbandry. London, 1727. 8vo.

—— Dictionarium Botanicum, or a Botanical Dictionary for
  the use of the Curious in Husbandry and Gardening.
  London, 1728. 2 vols. 8vo.
    " A work never before attempted."

—— The Riches of a Hop Garden explained. London,
  1729. 8vo.

—— A Dictionary of Plants, their description and use. London, 1747. 2 vols. 8vo.
>Bradley was also the author of several less important treatises on Gardening and Agriculture.

1707 JOHN MORTIMER. Whole Art of Husbandry, and Country-man's Kalendar. London, 1707. 8vo.

—— Part II, containing additions proper for the Husband-man and Gardener. London, 1712. 8vo.

—— Later editions, ed. by his grandson Thomas, 1716-1721 and 1761

WILLIAM FLEETWOOD, Bishop of St. Asaph and Ely. Curiosities of Nature and Art in Husbandry and Gardening. London, 1707. 8vo.   *
>Mentioned by Johnson.

CHARLES EVELYN. Ladies' Recreation; or the Pleasure and Profit of Gardening improved. London, 1707. 8vo.
>Several later editions, with slightly varying titles. That of 1719 is called Lady's Recreation or the Art of Gardening farther Improved.

1710 WILLIAM SALMON, M.D. The English Herbal, or History of Plants. London, 1710. Folio

1712 JOSEPH ADDISON. An Essay on the Pleasures of the Garden. (*The Spectator*, No. 477)

1713 ALEXANDER POPE. Essay on Verdant Sculpture. (*The Guardian*, No. 173)

JAMES PETIVER. A Catalogue of Mr. Ray's English Herbal, 1713-15. Folio   *

—— Historia naturalem, with 152 copper plates. London, 1764. 2 vols.
>Several papers in the Phil. Trans. relating to gardens in London, &c.

1714 JOHN LAWRENCE. The Clergyman's Recreation, shewing the pleasure and profit of the Art of Gardening. London, 1714. 8vo.
>Later editions, 1715, 1716; and the 5th, 1717.

—— The Gentleman's Recreation, &c. London, 1716. 8vo.

—— The Lady's Recreation; or the Art of Gardening improved . . . To which are added Observations concerning variegated greens by J. L. 1718. 8vo.

—— Gardening Improved (containing the three previous works). London, 1718. 8vo.

—— The Fruit Garden Kalendar. London, 1718. 8vo.

1714 —— A new System of Agriculture, being a complete book of Husbandry and Gardening, &c.   London, 1726. Folio

1715 G. CLARKE.   The Landed Man's Assistant.   1715.   12mo.*
Mentioned by Johnson.

STEPHEN SWITZER.   The Nobleman, Gentleman and Gardener's Recreation, &c.   London, 1715.   8vo.

—— Ichnographia Rustica.   London, 1718.   3 vols.   8vo.
This is an enlargement of the preceding work, second edition, 1741.

—— The Practical Fruit Gardener, &c.   London, 1724. 8vo.

—— Second edition, revised by Laurence and Bradley. London, 1731.   8vo.

—— A Compendious Method for raising of Italian Brocoli . . and other Foreign Kitchen Vegetables, &c. London, 1729.   8vo.
I have seen copies of this work dated 1729, called "third and revised edition," also "fourth edition," but I have never seen any of earlier date. Watt (and Johnson) mention a work called "A Compendious Method for raising Kitchen Vegetables," London, 1729, 8vo., which I am unable to trace, and conclude must be the same as this.

—— A Dissertation on the true Cythisus of the Ancients, &c.   London, 1731.   8vo.   *

C. J. WOLFE and JAMES GANDON.   Vitruvius Britannicus, or British Architect, containing plans, &c. of buildings and Gardens, public and private, in Great Britain; 200 copper-plates.   London, 1715

1716 REV. HENRY STEVENSON.   The Young Gardener's Director. London, 1716.   12mo.   *

—— The Gentleman Gardener instructed.   London, 1716. 12mo.   *
Mentioned by Johnson, who says the sixth edition is dated 1769.

1717 JOSEPH CARPENTER.   The Retir'd Gardener.   London, 1717.   8vo.

SAMUEL COLLINS.   Paradise Retrieved, or the Method of managing and improving Fruit Trees, with a Treatise on Melons and Cucumbers; 12 plates.   London, 1717.   8vo.

GEORGE ANDREW AGRICOLA.   The Artificial Gardener. London, 1717

—— Philosophical Treatise of Husbandry and Gardening. Translated by Bradley. London, 1721
—— On Planting. Edin. 1777
All three works translated from the German described by Watt.
GILES JACOB. The Country Gentleman's Vade-Mecum. 1717. 12mo.

1718 REV. JAMES GARDINER. Rapin of Gardens: a Latin Poem in 4 books, Englished by J. G. London, 1718.
See also Evelyn, 1658.

1720 PATRICK BLAIR, M.D. Botanick Essays. London, 1720. 8vo.
—— Pharmaco-Botanologia, or an alphabetical and classical Dissertation on all the British Indigenous and Garden Plants of the New London Dispensatory. London, 1723-28. 4to.

1722 THOMAS FAIRCHILD. The City Gardener, &c. London, 1722. 8vo.
—— The different and sometimes contrary motion of the sap in plants. Phil. Trans. 1724
—— Catalogus Plantarum. *See* Society of Gardeners, 1730
JOSEPH MILLAR or MILLER. Botanicum Officinale, or A Compendious Herbal. London, 1722. 8vo. *

1724 PHILIP MILLER. The Gardener's and Florist's Dictionary. London, 1724
—— Catalogus Plantarum Officinalium quæ in Horto Botanico Chelseiano atiextur. London, 1730
—— The Gardener's Dictionary. London, 1731-39. Folio
This was many times republished, abridged, translated, and enlarged. The second edition, 1733. In the seventh, 1759, Miller adopted the Linnean system of classification.
——The Gardener's Kalendar. London, 1732. 8vo.
Several later editions, the thirteenth dated 1782.
—— The Method of Cultivating Madder, &c. London, 1758 ·*
—— The Elements of Agriculture, translated from Duhamel du Monceau. 1764. 2 vols. 8vo.

1726 BATTY LANGLEY. Practical Geometry applied to the Arts of Building, Surveying, Gardening, &c. London, 1726. Folio
—— A Sure Method of improving Estates by plantations of Oak, Elm, Ash, Beech, &c. London, 1728. 4to. *
—— New Principles of Gardening, or the laying-out and planting Parterres. London, 1728. 4to.

1726 —— Pomona, or the Fruit Garden illustrated, &c. London,
          1729. Folio   .

—— The Landed Gentleman's Useful Companion (reprint
     of " A Sure Method," &c.). London, 1741

B. TOWNSEND. The Complete Seedsman. Shewing the best
     and easiest method for raising and cultivating every
     Sort of Seed, &c. 1726. 8vo.

The Gentleman Farmer, or certain observations on the
     Husbandry of Flanders, compared with that of
     England. 1726. 12mo. Anonymous   *
                    Mentioned by Johnson.

1727 S. J. The Vineyard ; a Treatise shewing the nature and
          method of planting, manuring, cultivating, and dress-
          ing Vines in foreign parts, &c. 1727   *
                    Mentioned by Johnson.

ROBERT FURBER. Catalogue of English and Foreign trees.
     London, 1727. 8vo.   *
                    Mentioned by Watt.

—— Fruits for every month in the year. 12 plates. 1732.
     8vo.   *

—— An Introduction to Gardening, &c. London, 1733.
     8vo.

1728 ROBERT CASTEL. The Villas of the Ancients, "illustrated
          with remarks and cuts." London, 1728. Folio   *

1729 JOHN COWELL. A true Account of the Aloe Americana, or
          Africana now in blossom . . . also two other exotic
          plants call'd the Cereus or Torch-thistle. London,
          1729. 8vo.

—— The Curious and Profitable Gardener. London, 1730.
     8vo.   *

—— The Curious Fruit and Flower Gardener. Second
     Edition. London, 1732. 8vo.
          Same work as above with different title-page.

1730 A SOCIETY OF GARDENERS. Catalogus Plantarum. A Cata-
          logue of trees, shrubs . . in the gardens near London.
          Part I (rest never published). London, 1730. Folio
          Thomas Fairchild's name appears first on the list of the twenty
          gardeners who signed the Preface, so this work is sometimes
          catalogued under his name, or under that of Philip Miller, whose
          name is also on the list.

1731 MARK CATESBY. Natural History of California, Florida, &c.
          &c. London, 1731. Imp. folio

—— Hortus Europæ Americanus, or a Collection of 85 Curious Trees and Shrubs, &c. London, 1767. 4to.

1732 An Essay concerning the best methods of pruning Fruit Trees, &c. London, 1732. 8vo. Anonymous *

The nature and method of planting, manuring, and dieting a Vineyard. London, 1732. 8vo. Anonymous *

The great Improvement of Commons that are enclosed for the advantage of Lords of the Manor, the Poor, and the Public, with methods of enriching all soils, and raising timber. To ripen fruit at all times of the year ; an improvement in raising Mushrooms, Cucumbers, &c. 1732. Anonymous *

These three anonymous works are mentioned by Johnson.

WILLIAM HARPER. A Sermon on Gardening, preached at Malpas, Co. of Chester, at a Meeting of Gardeners and Florists, April 18th, 1732. London, 1732. 4to.

The Flower Garden Displayed. London, 1732. 4to.

—— A Second Edition, to which is added "A Flower Garden for Gentlemen and Ladies, being the Art of raising Flowers . . . also salleting, cucumbers, &c. as it is now practised by Sir Thomas More. Above 400 curious representations of the most beautiful flowers, &c. from the designs of Mr. Furber and others, coloured to the Life. London, 1734. 4to.

WILLIAM ELLIS. Complete Modern Husbandry, containing the Practice of Farming, etc. Second Edition. London, 1732. 8vo.

—— The Practical Farmer or Hertfordshire Husbandman. London, 1732

—— The Timber Tree improved, or the best practical methods of improving different lands with proper timber. London, 1738

Ellis was the author of several other Agricultural Treatises.

1736 PLUCHÉ-HUMPHRYS. Nature Displayed, translated from the French of N. A. Pluché, by George Humphrys. London, 1736. 8vo.

1737 BLAKEWELL's Herbal. 1737

1738 PUBLIC GARDENS. Collection of notes about Ranelagh, Cuper's Garden, &c. (Guildhall Library.) 1738-46

1739 SAMUEL TROWELL. A New Treatise of Husbandry, Garden-
       ing and other curious matters relating to country
       affairs. London, 1739. 8vo.

—— The Farmer's Instructor or Husbandman, and Gar-
       dener's useful and necessary Companion. Ed. by
       William Ellis. 1747   *
                    Mentioned by Johnson.

An Essay upon Harmony, as it relates chiefly to situation
       and building. London, 1739. 8vo. Anonymous *

1740 CHRISTOPHER GRAY. A Catalogue of Trees and Shrubs . . .
       for sale. 1740   *

1744 Adam's Luxury and Eve's Cookery, or the Kitchen Garden
       displayed. London, 1744. 8vo.   `   *

Curious Experiments in Gardening, &c. 1744. 12mo.   *
             These four works are mentioned by Johnson.

JOHN WILSON. Synopsis of British Plants, in Ray's Method,
       with a Botanical Dictionary. Newcastle, 1744

1745 A Plan of Mr. Pope's Garden and Grotto, &c. 1745

1746 DAVID STEPHENSON, M.A. The Gentleman's Gardener's
       Director of Plants, Flowers, and Trees, with a
       Garden Kalendar. London, 1746. 8vo.   *

The Beauties of Stowe. London, 1746

A description of the Gardens of Lord Viscount Cobham at
       Stowe. Northampton, 1747

A dialogue upon the Gardens of Lord Viscount Cobham at
       Stowe. London, 1748. 8vo.

The Gardens of Lord Viscount Cobham at Stowe.
       London, 1751

GEORGE BICKHAM. The Beauties of Stowe. 1753. 8vo.

A description of the House and Gardens of the Marquis of
       Buckingham at Stowe. Buckingham, 1797

1747 The Complete Florist; 100 engravings. London, 1747.
       8vo. Anonymous

1748 SIR WILLIAM WATSON. Papers published in the Philo-
       sophical Transactions. Accounts of the remains of
       John Tradescant's Botanic Garden at Lambeth. 1750.
       Account of the Bishop of London's Garden at Fulham.
       1751. And several others on similar subjects.

—— A Letter to Andrew Ducarel. London, 1774. 4to.

1752 ATTIRET-BEAUMONT. An Account of the Emperor of China's Gardens at Pekin, by J. D. Attiret. Translated by Sir H. Beaumont, *i.e.* Joseph Spence. London, 1752

JAMES NEWTON. Compleat Herbal. London, 1752. 8vo.

1753 W. WEBB. A Catalogue of Seeds and Roots under their proper heads. 1753   *

FRANCIS COVENTRY. Essay in "The World" of April 12th, 1753 (No. XV.) entitled, "Strictures on the absurd novelties introduced in Gardening," and a humorous description of Squire Mushroom's Villa. 1753   *

BARTHOLOMEW ROCQUE. A Treatise on the Hyacinth, &c. London, 1753   *

—— A Practical Treatise on cultivating Lucerne-Grass, &c. London, 1775

1754 JAMES JUSTICE. The Scot's Gardener's Director. Edinburgh, 1754

—— The British Gardener's Director. Edinburgh, 1764. The Useful Herbal. Anonymous. London, 1754. 8vo.

1755 WILLIAM JOHN HALFPENNY. Rural Architecture in the Chinese taste. 1755. 8vo.

JOHN DALTON, D.D. Some thoughts on Building and planting, addressed to Sir James Lowther, Bart. London, 1755. 4to.

1756 On the Heat and Cold of Hot-houses. Anonymous. London, 1756. 8vo.   *

TIMOTHY SHELDRAKE (the elder). Gardener's Best Companion in a Greenhouse. London [c. 1756]. Folio

—— An Herbal of Medicinal Plants, etc. London [c. 1759]

JOHN HILL, M.D. (Sir J. H.). The British Herbal, an History of plants .. cultivated for use or raised for Beauty. London, 1756. Folio

1757 HALE. Eden, or a Complete Body of Gardening . . . compiled by Sir John Hill from the papers left by Hale. London, 1757. Folio

1757 THOMAS HITT. A Treatise of Fruit Trees. London, 1757.
8vo. (2nd ed.)   *

—— A Treatise of Husbandry on the improvement of dry
and barren lands. London, 1760. 8vo.

EDWARD LISLE. Observations on Husbandry. 1757. 4to.
Edited by his son, T. Lisle.

ROBERT MAXWELL. The practical Husbandman. 1757

WILLIAM MASON (the Poet). An heroic Epistle to Sir W.
Chambers. London, 1757. 4to.

—— An heroic Postscript. 1758

—— The English Garden, a Poem, in 4 books 8vo. 1772
Edition with Commentary and Notes, by W. Burgh. 1785.

JAMES THOMPSON. The distinguishing properties of a fine
Auricula. Newcastle, 1757. 8vo.

—— The Dutch Florist. Newcastle, 1758. 12mo.

FRANCIS HOME. Principles of Agriculture and Vegetation.
Edinburgh, 1757. 8vo.

1758 THOMAS BARNES. New method of Propagating Fruit Trees
and Shrubs, confirmed by repeated and successful
experience. London, 1758. 8vo.   *
Later editions, 1759 and 1762.

REV. WILLIAM HANBURY. An Essay on Planting, and a
scheme for making it conducive to the glory of God.
Oxford, 1758. " An 8vo. pamphlet "   *

—— A complete body of planting and gardening. London,
1770-1. Folio

1759 RICHARD NORTH. A Treatise on Grasses and the Norfolk
Willow. London, 1759. 8vo.

—— The Gardener's Catalogue of Hardy Trees, Shrubs,
Flowers, Seeds, &c. 1759. 8vo.   *
Mentioned by Johnson.

JOHN MILLS. Practical Treatise on Husbandry, translated
from the French of Duhamel de Monceau. 1759.
4to. With plates

—— A new and complete System of Practical Husbandry.
1762. 5 vols. 8vo.

—— The Natural and Chemical Elements of Agriculture,
from the German of Gyllenborg. 1770. 12mo.

—— Essays on Agriculture. 1772. 8vo.

BENJAMIN STILLINGFLEET. Miscellaneous Tracts relating to Natural History. Translated from the Latin of various Swedish authors. London, 1759. 8vo.

—— 2nd edition with the addition of the Calendar of Flora, from the Swedish of Berger. London, 1762. 8vo.

—— A Discourse concerning the irritability of some Flowers, from the Italian [1767]. 8vo.

1760 SAMUEL PULLEIN. Observations towards a method of preserving the seeds of Plants in a state of Vegetation during long voyages. London, 1760. 8vo.   *

JAMES LEE. An Introduction to Botany, containing an explication of the Theory of that Science, &c. London, 1760. 8vo.

—— Catalogue of Plants and Seeds sold by Kennedy and Lee, at the Vineyard, Hammersmith. 1774. 8vo.

The London Gardener. Anonymous. London, 1760. 8vo. *
 Mentioned by Johnson.

Adam Armed: or an Essay endeavouring to prove the advantages . . the kingdom may receive . . . by means of a well ordered and duly rectified Charter for incorporating and regulating the Professor of the Art of Gardening; humbly offered and presented by the Master and Company of the same. London. Folio
Johnson mentions this work and says it has no author's name or date, but was published about this year.

1762 T. LIGHTOLER. The Gentleman and Farmer's Architecture; being Plans for Parsonage and Farm Houses, with Pineries, Greenhouses, &c. With Plates. London, 1762. Folio
 Johnson mentions an edition of 1766.

1763 GEORGE RITSO. Kew Gardens: a Poem. London, 1763 *

JAMES WHEELER. The Botanists' and Gardeners' New Dictionary, containing names, classes, &c. . . according to the System of Linnæus. London, 1763. 8vo.

—— An Essay on the Theory of Agriculture, &c. London, 1763. 12mo.   *

THOMAS MARTYN, F.R.S. Plantae Cantabrigienses, or a Catalogue of Plants which grow wild in the County of Cambridge. London, 1763. 8vo.

—— A Short Account of the Donation to the Botanic Garden, by Dr. Walker. London, 1763. 4to.

3

1763 —— Catalogus Horti Botanici Cantabrigiensis, a Catalogue of the Botanic Garden at Cambridge. Cambridge, 1771. 8vo.

—— Rousseau's Letters; or the Elements of Botany, addressed to a Young Lady; with Notes, and twenty-four additional Letters, explaining the system of Linnæus. Translated from the French. London, 1785. 8vo.
5th edition, 1796.

—— Thirty-eight Plates, with Explanations intended to illustrate Linnæus' System of Vegetables, and particularly adapted to the Letters on the Elements of Botany. London, 1788. 8vo.

—— Flora Rustica, exhibiting figures of such Plants as are either useful or hurtful in Husbandry; with Scientific Characters, &c. London, 1792-4. 8vo.

—— The Language of Botany; being a Dictionary of the Terms made use of in that Science, principally by Linnæus, &c. London, 1793. 8vo.

—— The Gardeners' and Botanists' Dictionary of the late Philip Miller, corrected and newly arranged, with additions. London, 1803-7. 4 vols. folio

—— Various papers contributed to the Transactions of the Linnæan Society. 4to.

1764 REV. WALTER HARTE. Essays on Husbandry, and a Treatise on Lucerne, by W. H., Canon of Windsor. With plates. 1764 and 1770

The Dutch Florist, from the Dutch of Van Campen. 1764. 4to.   *

Museum Rusticum et Commerciale, &c. London, 1764. 6 vols. 8vo.   *

De Re Rustica. A similar work to the above, begun 1768, completed 1770. 2 vols. 8vo.   *
These three works are thus described by Johnson.

WILLIAM SHENSTONE. Unconnected Thoughts on Gardening, in Essays on Men and Manners. 1764. 3 vols. 8vo.

The Complete Farmer; or, Dictionary of Husbandry. Published by David Henry. 1764.
Johnson mentions a second edition, 1768.

1766 JOHN LOCKE. Observations upon the growth and culture of Vines and Olives, &c., from his original MS. in the possession of the Earl of Shaftesbury. London, 1766. 8vo.

1767 The rise and progress of the present Taste in planting Parks, Pleasure Grounds, Gardens, &c., from the time of Henry VIII. to George III. In a poetic epistle to the Right Hon. Charles, Lord Viscount Irwin. 1767

JAMES RUTTER and DANIEL CARTER. Modern Eden, or the Gardener's universal Guide, &c. London, 1767. 8vo. *

JOHN GILES. Ananas; or a Treatise on the Pine Apple, &c. To which is added the true method of raising the finest Melons with the greatest success, &c. London, 1767. 8vo.

GEO. DIONYSIUS EHRET, F.R.S. Of a new Peruvian Plant lately introduced into the English Gardens (the Nolana prostrata of Linnæus). Phil. Trans. 1767

JOHN ABERCROMBIE. Every Man his own Gardener. 1767. 12mo.

This work has the name of Thomas Mawe also on the title, and went through several later editions.

—— The Universal Gardener and Botanist, &c. London, 1778. 4to.

—— The Garden Mushroom, its Nature and Cultivation, &c. London, 1779. 8vo.

—— The British Fruit Garden, and Art of Pruning, &c. London, 1779. 8vo.

—— The Complete Forcing Gardener, &c. London, 1781. 12mo.

—— The Complete Wall-tree Pruner, &c. London, 1783. 12mo.

—— The Propagation and Botanical Arrangement of Plants and Trees, useful and ornamental. London, 1785. 2 vols. 12mo.

—— The Gardener's Pocket Dictionary, &c. London, 1786. 3 vols. 12mo.

—— Daily Assistant in the Modern Practice of English Gardening, &c. London, 1789. 12mo.

1767 —— The Universal Gardener's Kalendar, &c.   London,
1789. 12mo.

—— The Complete Kitchen Gardener, and Hot-bed Forcer,
&c. London, 1789. 12mo.

—— The Gardener's Vade-mecum, &c. London, 1789. 8vo.

—— The Hot-house Gardener, &c. London, 1789. 8vo.

—— The Gardener's Pocket Journal, &c. London, 1791.
12mo.

> Most of these works went through several editions.

1768 GEORGE MASON. An Essay on Design Gardening.
London, 1768. 8vo.

—— Revised edition. 1795

JOHN GIBSON, M.D. The Fruit Gardener, containing the
method of raising Stocks for multiplying Fruit
Trees, &c. London, 1768. 8vo.

> Presumably by J. Gibson, although his name does not appear on
> the title-page.

THOMAS WILDMAN. A Treatise on the culture of Peach
Trees, to which is added a Treatise on the management of Bees. 1768

1769 JAMES GARTON. The Practical Gardener and Gentleman's
Directory for every month in the year, &c. London,
1769. 12mo.

ANTHONY POWELL. The Royal Gardener, or complete
Calendar of Gardening for every month in the year, &c.
London, 1769. 12mo.   *

ADAM TAYLOR. A Treatise on the Anana, or Pine Apple, &c.
Devizes, 1769. 8vo.

THE HON. DAINES BARRINGTON. On the Trees which are
supposed to be Indigenous in Great Britain. 1769

—— Chestnut Trees not Indigenous in Great Britain. 1771

—— Mr. Pegge's Observations on the Growth of the Vine in
England, considered and answered. 1777

—— On the Progress of Gardening, in a letter to Mr. Norris,
1782.

> These treatises are all published in the Archæologia.

RICHARD WESTON. Tracts on practical Agriculture and
Gardening . . . to which is added, a Complete
Chronological Catalogue of English Authors on
Agriculture, Gardening, &c. London, 1769. 8vo.

—— Second edition, greatly enlarged. 1773
The author's name appears in this but not in the first edition.

—— Botanicus universalis et hortulanus, &c. 4 vols.
London, 1770-1777. 8vo.

—— The Gardener's and Planter's Calendar. London, 1773.
8vo.

—— The Gardener's Pocket Calendar. (2nd ed.) London,
Bell's edition. No date, about 1779. 12mo.

—— Flora Anglicana. London, 1775-89. 8vo.

—— A new cheap Manure . . . Alabaster or gypsum.
Leicester, 1791. 8vo.

1770 HORACE WALPOLE. Essay on Modern Gardening, written
in 1770, printed with a French translation on opposite
pages by the Duc de Nivernois. Strawberry Hill,
1785. 4to.

JOHN DOVE. Strictures on Agriculture, wherein a discovery
of the Physical course of Vegetation, of the Food of
Plants, and the Rudiments of Tillage, is attempted.
London, 1770. 12mo.

LINNÆUS – MILNE. Institutes of Botany; containing
accurate, compleat, and easy Descriptions of all the
known Genera of Plants; from the Latin of Charles
Van Linné, by Rev. Colin Milne, LL.D. London,
1770. 4to.

A Botanical Dictionary; or, Elements of Systematic and
Philosophical Botany, etc. London, 1770. 8vo.
2nd edition, 1777. Supplement, 1778. 3rd and
enlarged edition, 1805. 8vo.

The Gardener's Alphabetical Calendar. 1770. 12mo.   *

The Pocket Kitchen Gardener. 1770. 12mo.   *

The Pocket Flower Gardener. 1770. 12mo.   *
These three works, without authors' names, are mentioned by
Johnson.

1770 THOMAS WHEATLEY, or WHATELY.   Observations on Modern Gardening, illustrated by descriptions. London, 1770. 8vo.

> Several later editions—the 5th, 1793.

JOHN ELLIS. Directions for bringing over Seeds and Plants from the East Indies and other distant Countries in a state of Vegetation. London, 1770. 4to.

—— Description of the Mangostan and Bread Fruit Tree. London, 1775. 4to.

—— An Historical Account of Coffee. With engravings and botanical descriptions of the tree . . . its culture and use. London, 1774. 4to.

1771 MATTHEW PETERS. The Rational Farmer, or a Treatise on Agriculture and Tillage. London, 1771. 8vo.

JAMES MEADER. The Modern Gardener or Universal Kalendar . . . from the Diary and MSS. of the late Mr. Flitt, corrected and improved by J. M.   London, 1771. 12mo.   *

—— The Planter's Guide or Pleasure Gardener's Companion. London, 1779. Oblong 8vo.

JOHN DICKS. The New Gardener's Dictionary, or the whole Art of Gardening fully and accurately displayed. London, 1771. Folio.

> An edition of 1769 is mentioned by Watt.

JOHN REINHOLD FORSTER, LL.D. Florae Americae Septentrionalis, or A Catalogue of the Plants of North America. London, 1771. 8vo.

—— Characteres generum Plantarum, quas in itinere ad insulas Maris Australis, illegerunt, descripserunt, et delineaverunt annis 1772-3. London, 1776. 4to.

1772 LOUIS DE ST. PIERRE. The Art of planting and cultivating the Vine, &c. according to the most approved methods in France. London, 1772. 12mo.

SIR WILLIAM CHAMBERS. A Dissertation on Oriental Gardening. London, 1772. 4to.

> The second, being the only other edition, 1773.

1773 ANDREW COLTEE DUCAREL, LL.B. and LL.D. A Letter to Wm. Watson, M.D., upon the early Cultivation of Botany in England; and some particulars about John Tradescant, Gardener to King Charles I. London, 1773. 4to.

1774 JOHN COAKLEY LETTSOM. Hortus Uptoneniis. A Catalogue of Dr. Fothergill's garden at Upton at the time of his decease. (No date) c. 1774. 8vo.

—— Grovehill, a rural and horticultural sketch. 1784. 4to.

—— A translation of Abbé de Commerell's account of the culture of the Mangel Wurzel or Root of Scarcity. London, 1788.

1775 LINNÆUS—JENKINSON. A Generic and Specific Description of British Plants; translated from the Genera et Species Plantarum, of Linnæus; with Notes and Observations, by James Jenkinson. Kendal, 1775. 8vo.

REV. SAMUEL WARD. A Modern System of Natural History, containing accurate descriptions and faithful histories of animals, vegetables, and minerals. London, 1775-77. 12 vols. 12mo.   *

—— An Essay on the different natural Situations of Gardens. London, 1775. 4to.   *

1776 HENRY HOME, LORD KAMES. The Gentleman Farmer. Edinburgh, 1776. 8vo.
Several later editions—the sixth in 1815.

WILLIAM WITHERING, M.D., F.R.S., F.L.S. A Botanical Arrangement of all the Vegetables naturally growing in Great Britain, with an easy Introduction to the Study of Botany. (Plates.) Birm. 1776. 2 vols. 8vo.

—— 2nd edition. London, 1778-90. 3 vols.   *

—— 3rd edition. 1796. 4 vols.   *

1777 JAMES ANDERSON, LL.D. Thoughts on Planting (first appeared in the Edinburgh Weekly Magazine), by Agricola. Edin. 1777. 8vo.   *

—— A Description of a Patent Hot-house, &c. London, 1804. 12mo.

WILLIAM WILSON. A Treatise on the forcing of Early Fruits, and the management of Hot Walls. London, 1777. 12mo.

CONRAD LODDIGE's Catalogue of Plants and Seeds sold by C. L . . at Hackney near London. 1777. 8vo.
The names of plants are in German as well as in English.

1777 —— The Botanical Cabinet. London, 1818-33. 20 vols. 8vo.

JOSEPH HEELEY.   Letter on the Beauties of Hagley, Envil and the Leasowes, etc.   London, 1777.   12mo.

—— Description of Hagley Park.   London, 1777.   8vo.

JOHN KENNEDY.   A Treatise upon Planting, Gardening, and the Management of the Hot-house.   2nd ed., enlarged. London, 1777.   2 vols. 8vo.

1778 The Practical Gardener, &c.   London, 1778.   No author's name   *

N. SWINDEN.   The Beauties of Flora displayed, &c.   London, 1778.   8vo.

1779 ADAM NEALE.   A Catalogue of Plants in the garden of John Blackburne, Esq., at Orford, Lancashire, alphabetically arranged, according to the Linnean system. Warrington, 1779.   8vo.

WILLIAM SPEECHLEY.   A Treatise on the cultivation of the Pine Apple.   York, 1779.   8vo.

—— A Treatise on the culture of the Vine in England. York, 1790.   4to.

THOMAS ELLIS (gardener to the Bishop of London).   The Gardener's Pocket Calendar.   London, 1779.   12mo.
An earlier edition is said to have been published anonymously in 1770.

JOHN MILLER.   An Illustration of the Sexual System of Linnæus.   London, 1779.   2 vols. 8vo.

A General Dictionary of Husbandry, Planting, Gardening, and the Vegetable part of the Materia Medica . . . . selected from the best authors by the Editors of the Farmers' Magazine.   Bath, 1779.   2 vols. 8vo.

1780 ALEXANDER WILSON, M.D.   Some Observations relating to the Influence of Climate on Vegetables and Animal Bodies.   London, 1780.   8vo.

JOHN TRUSLER.   Practical Husbandry.   1780.   8vo.

—— Elements of Modern Gardening.   8vo.
The title-page has neither name nor date.   The B.M. Catalogue ascribes it to Trusler, and assigns it to the year 1800.   Johnson does not give any author, and dates it 1784.

1781 WILLIAM HOUSTOUN, D.D.   Reliquiæ Houstounianæ, a Catalogue and Description of Plants.   1781.   4to.
Published by Sir Joseph Banks.

SAMUEL FULLMER. The Young Gardener's best Companion for the Kitchen and Fruit Garden. London, 1781. 12mo.

1782 WILLIAM RALEY. A Treatise on the Management of Potatoes. London, 1782. 8vo.

1783 ERMENONVILLE—MALTHUS. An Essay on Landscape. From the French of Ermenonville. 1783. 12mo.　　*
No author's name, but said by Johnson to be by Mr. Malthus.

CHARLES BRYANT. Flora Diætetica, or History of Esculent Plants, &c. London, 1783. 8vo.

—— A Dictionary of the Ornamental Trees, &c. Norwich, 1790. 8vo.

DE LILLE.—On Gardening. Translated from the French of l'Abbé de Lille. 1783. 4to.　　*

WILLIAM FALCONER, M.D., F.R.S. An Historical View of the Taste for Gardening and Laying out Grounds among the Nations of Antiquity. 1783. 8vo.　　*

—— An Essay on the Preservation of the Health of Persons employed in Agriculture, &c. Bath, 1789. 8vo.

—— Miscellaneous Tracts and Collections relating to Natural History, &c. Cambridge, 1793. 4to.

THOMAS KYLE. A Treatise on the Management of Peach and Nectarine Trees, either in forcing-houses, or on hot and common walls. Edinburgh, 1783. 8vo.

—— Catalogue of Plants, with their English and Latin Linnæan names, sold by Lucker and Smith, Dalston. 1783. 8vo.

WILLIAM GILPIN. Observations . . . relative chiefly to Picturesque Beauty. 1783 to 1809. 11 separate vols. 8vo.
Several distinct works, descriptive of Tours in different parts of England, containing accounts of gardens, &c.

1785 SAMUEL FELTON. Miscellanies on Ancient and Modern Gardening, and on the Scenery of Nature. London, 1785. 8vo.　　*
Without author's name.

—— On the Portraits of English Authors on Gardening. London, 1828. 8vo.

1785 —— Gleanings on Gardens, chiefly respecting the ancient style in England. London, 1829. 8vo.

WILLIAM MARSHALL. Planting and Ornamental Gardening : a Practical Treatise. London, 1785. 8vo.
Without author's name.

—— 2nd edition, with the title Planting and Rural Ornament. London, 1796. 8vo.

JAMES BOLTON. Filices Britanniæ, an History of the British proper Ferns, with plain and accurate Descriptions, &c. Leeds, 1785

JOHN, EARL OF BUTE. Botanical Tables, containing the different families of British Plants, &c. London, 1785. 9 vols. 8vo.   *

JAMES DICKSON, F.L.S. Fasciculus Plantarum Cryptogamicarum Britanniæ. London, 1785
Dickson was the author of many papers in the Horticultural Society's Transactions.

1786 FRANCIS XAVIER VISPRE. A Dissertation on the growth of Wine in England. Bath, 1786. 8vo.

ROBERT BROWNE. A Method to preserve Peach and Nectarine Trees from the effect of Mildew, &c. London, 1786. 12mo.

REV. PHILIP LE BROCQ, M.A. A Description of certain methods of Planting, Training, and Managing all kinds of Fruit Trees, Vines, &c. London, 1786. 8vo.

—— A Sketch of a Plan for making the Tract of Land called the New Forest a real Forest, and for various other purposes of the first national importance. 1793. 8vo.

The Compleat Herbal, or Family Physician, giving an account of all such Plants as are now used in the Practice of Physic, with their Descriptions and Virtues. 2 vols. No author's name. London, 1787. 8vo.

1787 WILLIAM CURTIS. The Botanical Magazine (begun by). London, 1787
First series, 1787 to 1826, 53 vols.; Index, 1828. Second series, edited by S. Curtis and W. J. Hooker, 1827 to 1844, 17 vols. Third series, edited by Sir W. J. Hooker, 1845 to 1858, 13 vols.

—— Flora Londinensis. 1777-1828. 5 vols. folio

GEORGE WINTER. A new and compendious System of Husbandry, containing the mechanical, chemical, and philosophical Elements of Agriculture. Bristol, 1787. 8vo.

1788 SIR JAMES EDWARD SMITH. Some observations on the irritability of Vegetables. London, 1788. 4to.

—— Plantarum Icones hactenus ineditæ, plerumque ad Plantas in Herbario Linnæno conservatus delineatæ. London, 1789-91. Folio

—— Icones Pictae Plantarum rariorum descriptionibus . . illustratae. London, 1790-93. Folio

—— Spicilegium Botanicum. Gleanings in Botany. London, 1791-2. Folio

—— A Specimen of the Botany of New Holland. The figures by J. Sowerby. London, 1793. 4to. (only 1 vol. published)

—— Syllabus of a Course of Lectures on Botany. London, 1795. 8vo.

—— Remarks on the Generic Character of the Decandrons Papalionaceous Plants of New Holland. London, 1804. 8vo.

—— Exotic Botany . . . coloured figures . . of such new, beautiful or rare plants as are worthy of cultivation in the Gardens of Britain. The figures by J. Sowerby. London, 1804-5. 2 vols. 4to.

—— An Introduction to Physiological and Systematic Botany. London, 1807. 8vo.

—— Review of the Modern State of Botany, etc. Edinburgh, 1817. 4to.

—— A Grammar of Botany. London, 1821. 8vo.

1789 JOHN GRAEFER. A Descriptive Catalogue of upwards of 1100 species and varieties of Herbaceous Plants, &c., with a List of Hardy Ferns, &c., &c. London, 1789. 8vo. *

1789 JAMES ADAM. Practical Essays on Agriculture, containing an Account of Soils, and the manner of correcting them; an Account of the culture of all Field Plants; also on the Culture and management of Grass Lands, &c. London, 1789. 2 vols. 8vo.   *

WILLIAM AITON. Hortus Kewensis. London, 1789. 3 vols. 8vo.

—— Second edition enlarged by his son, William Townsend Aiton, 1810-13. 5 vols. 8vo.

1790 RICHARD PULTENEY. Historical and biographical sketches of the progress of Botany. London, 1790. 2 vols. 8vo.

—— General View of the Writings of Linnæus. London, 1805. 4to.

—— Decorations for Plants and Garden. Published by Taylor. Cir. 1790

E. O. DONOVAN, F.R. and L.S. The Botanical Review, or the Beauties of Flora. Nos. 1-7. London, 1790

BRULLES. Hints for the management of Hot-beds, &c. Bath, 1790. 8vo.   *

WILLIAM WOODVILLE, M.D. Medical Botany. London, 1790. 3 vols. Supplement. James Phillips. 1794. 4to.

1791 RICHARD ANTHONY SALISBURY. Icones Stirpium variorum, Descriptionibus illustratae. London, 1791. 8vo.

—— Paradisus Londinensis. London, 1805-8. 4to.
     Salisbury contributed many valuable papers to the Trans. Horticultural Society.

ERASMUS DARWIN, M.D., F.R.S. The Botanic Garden, a poem, in two parts : part I, The Economy of Vegetation; part II, The Loves of the Plants. London, 1791. 4to.

—— Phytologia, or the Philosophy of Agriculture and Gardening, &c. London, 1800. 4to.

JAMES SOWERBY, F.L.S. The Florist's Delight, &c. London, 1791. Folio

—— Figures of English Fungi, or Mushrooms. London, 1792-1803. 3 vols. folio

—— English Botany, with Sir J. E. Smith, 1790-1820. 36 vols. 8vo.

WILLIAM FORSYTH, F.A.S. Observations on the Diseases, Defects, and Injuries in all kinds of Fruit and Forest Trees, &c. London, 1791. 8vo.

—— A Treatise on the culture and management of Fruit Trees, &c. London, 1802. 4to.

1792 The Linnæan Society's Transactions, first published. 1791. 8vo.

Among the contributors of papers on Gardening subjects in the early numbers are the following: C. C. Babington, H. T. Cole-brooke, Peter Collinson, L. W. Dillwyn, R. K. Greville, W. J. Hooker, J. Lindley, T. Martyn, R. Rudge, J. E. Smith, J. Sowerby, C. Stevens, J. Woods.

JAMES MADDOCK. Florist's Directory and Treatise on the Culture of Flowers, &c. London, 1792. 8vo.

—— An improved edition by J. Curtis. London, 1810. 8vo.

1793 RICHARD STEELE. An Essay on Gardening, containing a Catalogue of Exotic Plants, &c. York, 1793. 4to. *

1794 WILLIAM AMOS. The Theory and Practice of Drill Husbandry. London, 1794. 4to. *

—— Minutes of Agriculture and Planting. London, 1804. 4to.

ADRIAN HARDY HAWORTH. Observations on the genus Mesembryanthemum. London, 1794. 8vo.

—— Synopsis Plantarum Succulentarum, &c. London, 1812-19. 8vo.

SAMUEL HAYES, M.R.L.A. A practical Treatise on Planting. Dublin, 1794. 8vo.

JAMES SHAW. Plans, elevations, sections, observations, and explanations of Forcing houses in Gardening. Whitby, 1794. Folio

JAMES McPHAIL. A Treatise on the Culture of the Cucumber, &c. London, 1794. 8vo.

—— The Gardener's Remembrancer throughout the year, &c. London, 1803. 8vo.

WILLIAM MAUNSELL, LL.D. Letter on the Culture of Potatoes from the Shoots. London, 1794. 8vo.

SIR UVEDALE PRICE. An Essay on the Picturesque, as compared with the sublime and beautiful, &c. London, 1794-98. 8vo.

1794 —— A Letter to H. Repton, Esq., on the application of the practice, as well as the principles of Landscape Painting, to Landscape Gardening, &c. London, 1795. 8vo.

—— A Dialogue on the distinct characters of the Picturesque and the Beautiful, in answer to the objections of Mr. Knight. London, 1801

—— On the Picturesque; including A Letter to H. Repton, Esq., and On Decorations near the House. Edited by Sir Thomas Dick Lauder. London, 1842

HUMPHRY REPTON. A Letter to Uvedale Price, Esq. on Landscape Gardening. London, 1794. 4to.

—— Sketches and Hints on Landscape Gardening, &c. London, 1795. Folio

—— Observations on the Theory and Practice of Landscape Gardening, &c. London, 1803. 4to.

—— An Enquiry into the changes in Landscape Gardening. London, 1806. 8vo.

—— On the introduction of Indian Architecture and Gardening. London, 1808. Folio   *

—— On the supposed effects of Ivy on Trees. Trans. Linn. Soc. London, 1810   *

—— Fragments on the Theory and Practice of Landscape Gardening. London, 1817. Folio

RICHARD PAYNE KNIGHT. The Landscape; a Didactic Poem, in 3 books, addressed to Uvedale Price, Esq. 1794. 4to.

—— Review of the Landscape; also of an Essay on the Picturesque; with Practical Remarks on Rural Ornament. 1795. 8vo.

1795 WILLIAM ROXBURGH, M.D., F.R.S. Plants of the Coast of Coromandel, &c. London, 1795

1796 FRANCIS BAUER. Delineation of Exotick Plants cultivated in the Royal Garden at Kew, drawn and coloured, and the botanical characters displayed, according to the Linnæan System. London, 1796. Folio

—— Illustrationes Floræ Novæ Hollandiæ, &c. Part I. 1813   *

REV. CHARLES MARSHALL. Introduction to the Knowledge and Practice of Gardening; with Hints on Fish Ponds. London, 1796. 12mo.
Several later editions—the third, 1800.

GEORGE LINDLEY. The plan of an Orchard, exhibiting at one view a select quantity of Trees, &c. 1796 *
Described by Johnson as a folio sheet.

—— An Account of the Culture of Potatoes in Ireland. 1796. 8vo. *
These two works are mentioned by Johnson.

JAMES DON. Hortus Cantabrigensis, a Catalogue of Plants Indigenous and Exotic. 1796. 8vo.

1797 STRICKLAND FREEMAN. Select Specimens of British Plants. Five plates. London, 1797. Folio
Part II. contains descriptions of the plants by G. Shaw.

FRANCIS DUCKENFIELD ASTLEY. A few minutes' advice to Gentlemen of landed Property, and the admirers of Forest Scenery, &c., &c. Chester, 1797. 12mo. *

—— Hints to Planters, from various Authors of esteemed Authority. Manchester, 1807. 8vo. *

THOMAS SKIP DYOT BUCKNAL. The Orchardist, &c., &c. London, 1797. 8vo.

THOMAS ANDREW KNIGHT, F.R.S. A Treatise on the Culture of the Apple and Pear, and on the manufacture of Cyder and Perry. London, 1797. 12mo.

—— Some Doubts relative to the efficacy of Mr. Forsyth's Plaister, in renovating Trees. London, 1802. 4to.

—— Report of a Committee of the Horticultural Society of London. London, 1805. 4to.

—— A Letter on the origin of Blight, &c. London, 1806

—— Pomona Herefordiensis, or a descriptive account of the old Cyder and Perry Fruits of Herefordshire. London, 1811. 4to.
Knight was the author of numerous papers in Trans. Hort. Soc. and other periodicals.

WILLIAM SALISBURY. Hortus Paddingtonensis, &c. London, 1797. 8vo.

—— The Botanist's Companion, &c. London, 1816. 12mo.

1797 —— Hints to the Proprietors of Orchards. 1817. 12mo.

—— The Cottager's Agricultural Companion, &c. 1822.
12mo.

—— Also Essay on packing Plants for exportation   *
Nicholson's Journal, XXX., p. 339.

WALTER NICOL. The Scotch Forcing Gardener, &c. Edinburgh, 1797. 8vo.

—— Practical Planter, &c. Edinburgh, 1799. 8vo.

—— Villa Garden Directory, &c. Edinburgh, 1809. 8vo.

—— Gardener's Kalendar, &c. Edinburgh, 1810. 8vo. *

—— Planter's Kalendar, &c. Edinburgh, 1812. 8vo.

HENRY ANDREWS. The Botanist's Repository, &c. Edinburgh, 1797-99. 4to.

—— A Review of Plants hitherto figured in the Botanist's
Repository. Edinburgh, 1801. 4to.   *

—— Engravings of Ericas or Heaths, with Botanical
descriptions. London, 1802. Folio

—— The Heathery, or Monograph of the genus Erica,
monthly numbers, in 6 vols. London, 1804 and 1814

—— Geraniums. London, 1805. 4to.

1798 CLEMENT ARCHER, M.R.L.A. Miscellaneous Observations
on the effect of Oxygen on the Animal and Vegetable
Systems, &c. Bath, 1798. 8vo.

ROBINSON. Forms of Stoves for Forcing Houses. London, 1798. 8vo.   *

1799 ROBERT JOHN THORNTON. A new Illustration of the Sexual
System of Linnæus. 1799

—— The Temple of Flora. 1805. Imperial folio
Beautifully engraved titles and coloured plates.

—— Family Herbal. (Engravings by Bewick.) 1810

—— Botanical Extracts, or Philosophy of Botany. (3 vols.)
1810

LADY CHARLOTTE MURRAY. British Garden. Bath, 1799. 8vo.

1800 WILLIAM PONTEY. The profitable Planter, &c. Hudders-
field, 1800. 12mo.

—— The Forest Pruner, &c. London, 1805. 12mo.

—— The Rural Improver. London, 1822

MRS. MONTOLIEU. The Enchanted Plants, Fables in Verse. London, 1808. 8vo.

—— The Gardens, a Poem. From the French of L'Abbé J. de Lille. 1805. 8vo.

REV. THOMAS OWEN, M.A. The Three Books of M. Terentius Varro, concerning Agriculture, translated into English. London, 1800. 8vo.

—— Agricultural Pursuits, translated from the Greek. London, 1805. 8vo.

—— Translation of the 14 Books of Palladius on Agriculture. London, 1807. 8vo.

1802 WILLIAM TURTON, M.D., F.L.S. A General System of Nature through the three grand kingdoms of Animals, Vegetables, and Minerals. Translated from Gmelin's last edition of the Systema Naturæ of Linnæus. 1802-6. 7 vols. 8vo.

Rural Recreations, or the Gardener's Instructor, &c. By a Society of Practical Gardeners. With plates. London, 1802. 8vo.

1803 JOHN CLAUDIUS LOUDON. Observations on laying out the Public Squares of London in the Literary Journal. 1803   *

—— Observations on the formation and management of useful and ornamental Plantations, &c. Edin., 1804. 8vo.

—— A short Treatise on some improvements lately made in Hot-houses. Edin., 1805. 8vo.

—— A Treatise on forming, improving, and managing Country Residences, &c. London, 1806. 2 vols. 4to.

—— Hints on the formation of Gardens and Pleasure Grounds, &c. 1812. 4to.

—— Remarks on the Construction of Hot-houses, &c. 1817. 4to.

—— Sketches of Curvilinear Hot-houses, &c. 1818

—— A comparative view of the Curvilinear, and common mode of Roofing Hot-houses. London, 1818. Folio *

4

1803 —— The Encyclopædia of Gardening. London, 1822. 8vo.
This work went through several later editions.

—— The different modes of cultivating the Pine Apple, &c.
London, 1822. 8vo.

—— The Encyclopædia of Plants. London, 1838. 8vo.
Loudon was the author of several other works and numerous treatises, and editor of the Gardener's Magazine, &c. MRS. LOUDON also was the author of many works on Gardening, among which are the following :—

—— Flower Garden of Ornamental Annuals. London, 1840. 4to.

—— Ladies' Companion to Flower Garden. London, 1841. 12mo.

—— Ladies' Country Companion. London, 1846. 12mo.

—— British Wild Flowers. London, 1846. 4to.

—— The Amateur Gardener's Calendar. London, 1857

1804 R. W. DICKSON, M.D. Practical Agriculture, or a Complete System of Modern Husbandry, &c. London, 1804 and 1805. 4to.
Editor of the Agricultural Magazine from July, 1807, to December, 1809.

1805 EDWARD RUDGE, F.L.S. Plantarum Guianæ rariarum, Icones et Descriptiones. London, 1805-7. 4 vols. folio

1806 WILLIAM GRIFFIN. Treatise on the cultivation of the Pine Apple. Newark, 1806. 8vo.
Another edition. 1810.

JOHN SIBTHORPE. Flora Græca, 1806-1840. 10 vols. folio

MRS. HENRIETTA M. MORIARTY. Viridarium; or Green House Plants. London, 1806. 8vo.

W. WALLIS MASON. Experiments on the Culture of Carrots.*
Nicholson's Journal, XV., p. 57. 1806.

1807 WILLIAM SHAW. The Practical Gardener. London, 1807.
8vo.   *

ALEXANDER MACDONALD. A complete Dictionary of practical Gardening. 1807. 2 vols. 4to.
Johnson says the author of this was R. W. Dickson (*see* 1804), and that Macdonald was an assumed name.

WILLIAM WATSON. On the Culture of Turnips   *
Nicholson's Journal, XVI., p. 14.

1809 J. ACTON. On the Germination of Seeds, in a letter. 1809.*
Nicholson's Journal, XXIII., p. 214.

JAMES DEDE. The English Botanist's Pocket Companion, containing the essential Generic characters of every British Plant, arranged agreeably to the Linnæan system. London, 1809. 12mo.

JOSEPH KNIGHT. An Essay on the cultivation of the Plants belonging to the Order of Proteæ. London, 1809. 4to.

MRS. AGNES IBBETSON. Many Contributions to Nicholson's Journal, on Plants and Seeds, &c. 1809 *

SYDENHAM EDWARDS. Sixty-one Plates, representing about 150 rare plants. London, 1809. 4to. *

—— The Botanical Register, or Ornamental Flower Garden and Shrubbery. 1815-1827. 8vo. 33 vols. (including index)

The continuation to 1847 was edited by J. Lindley.

1810 THOMAS HAYNES. Improved System of Nursery Gardening. London, 1810. 8vo.

—— Interesting Discoveries in Horticulture, being an easy system of Propagating American and Bog Soil Plants, &c. London, 1810. 8vo.

—— A Treatise on the improved culture of the Strawberry, Raspberry, and Gooseberry. London, 1812. 8vo.

—— On collecting Soils, and composts. London, 1812. 12mo.

1811 PETER LINDEGAARD. On the mode of forcing the Vine in Denmark. London, 1811. 8vo. *

Mentioned by Johnson.

1812 TRANSACTIONS of the Horticultural Society begun in 1812. First Series, 4to. 7 vols. 1812 to 1830. Second Series. 1835 to 1848. With general index

The following are among the Authors of the articles in the early volumes:—Sir J. Banks; J. Braddick; Sir B. Boothby; A. Carlisle; J. Dickson; J. Dunbar; J. Fairweather; Fuller; Sir H. Goodriche; C. Harrison; A. K. Haworth; A. Hawkins; J. Hayward; D. Hill; S. Jeeves; D. Judd; M. Keens; W. Kent; T. A. Knight; J. Lindley; G. Loddiges; Lutterel; J. Maher; H. S. Matthews; J. Mean; W. Morgan; C. H. Noehden; J. Sabine; R. A. Salisbury; A. Seton; A. Sherbrook; J. Simpson; W. Spence; J. Turner; J. Venables; J. Warre; J. Wedgewood; R. Wilbraham; T. Wilkinson; J. Williams; J. Wilmot.

4 *

1812 GEORGE BROOKSHAW.   Pomona   Britannica, or Correct
        Delineations of British Fruits, with Descriptions.
        Atlas folio.   London, 1812.

—— another edition.   Elephant 4to.   1817.   2 vols.

—— A Treatise on Flower Painting.   (Part I.)   1816.
        4to.   *

—— The Horticultural Repository, &c.   1817.   8vo.

JOSEPH TAYLOR.   Arbores Mirabiles, or a Description of the
        most remarkable Trees, Plants, and Shrubs in all
        parts of the World.   Illustrated.   London, 1812.
        12mo.

—— The Bible Garden.   A brief Description of all the trees
        and plants mentioned in Holy Scripture.   London,
        1836.   16mo.

THOMAS HOGG.   A concise and practical Treatise on the
        growth and culture of the Carnation, Pink, Auricula,
        Polyanthus, Ranunculus, Tulip, &c.   London, 1812.
        12mo.
                Second edition.   London, 1822.   12mo.

GEORGE TODD.   Plans, Elevations, and Sections of Hot-
        houses, &c.   London, 1812.   Folio   *

1813 PETER LYON.   Observations on the barrenness of Fruit
        Trees ; the means of prevention and cure.   Edin-
        burgh, 1813.   8vo.

—— A Treatise on the Physiology and Pathology of Trees,
        &c.   Edinburgh, 1816.   8vo.

—— Comely Garden, Edinburgh.   *
                Mentioned by Watt.

1814 JOHN CUSHING.   The Exotic Gardener.   London, 1814.
        8vo.
                Third edition.   1826.   8vo.

JOHN LUNAN (of the Island of Jamaica).   Hortus Jamai-
        censis, or a Botanical Description of Indigenous
        Plants and Exotics growing in the Island of Jamaica.
        London, 1814.   2 vols. 4to.

LEONARD PHILLIPS, JUN.   A Catalogue of Fruit Trees for
        sale.   London, 1814.   Folio   *

—— Transactions in the Fruit Tree Nursery, Vauxhall.
London, 1815. Folio   *

E. WEEKS. The Forcer's Assistant, &c., &c. Chipping
Norton, 1814. 8vo.   *

SIR JOHN SINCLAIR. General Report of the Agricultural
state, and Political circumstances of Scotland. Edinburgh, 1814. 8vo.

—— Account of some experiments to promote the improvement of Fruit Trees, by peeling the bark. London,
1820. 8vo.

FREDERICK PURSH. Flora Americana Septentrionalis, or a
Systematic Arrangement and Description of the
Plants of North America. London, 1814. 8vo.

1816 MARIA E. JACKSON. The Florist's Manual. ("By a Lady.")
London, 1816. 12mo.

J. SALTER. A Treatise upon Bulbous Roots, &c, Bath,
1816. 12mo.   *

GEORGE SINCLAIR. Hortus Gramineus Woburnensis, &c.
London, 1816. Folio

—— Hortus Ericaeus Woburnensis. London, 1825. 4to.*

—— An Essay on the Weeds of Agriculture. London, 1826.
8vo.

ISAAC EMMERTON. A plain and practical Treatise on the
culture and management of the Auricula, &c. London,
1816   *

—— —— second edition. London, 1819. 8vo.

JAMES MEAN. The Practical Gardener. London, 1817.
12mo.

1817 —— The Gardener's Companion. London, 1818. 12mo.
    Both works by John Abercrombie, edited and enlarged by James
    Mean.

W. B. PAGE. Page's Prodromus, or a general nomenclature
of all the plants, indigenous and exotic, cultivated in
the Southampton Botanic Gardens, &c. London,
1817. 8vo.

HENRY SMITH. Flora Sarisburiensis . . . delineation from
Nature of English Plants with their uses in Medicine,
the Arts, and Agriculture. Salisbury, 1817. 8vo.

The Shrubbery Almanack (a single sheet). 1818   *

1818 WILLIAM HOOKER (Botanic painter). Pomona Londinensis.
London, 1818. Folio

1818 JOSEPH HAYWARD. The Science of Horticulture. London, 1818. 8vo.

—— The Science of Agriculture. London, 1825. 8vo.

ROBERT SWEET, F.L.S. Hortus Suburbanus Londinensis, &c. London, 1818. 8vo.

—— The Hot-house and Green-house Manual, &c. London, 1820. 8vo.   *

—— —— second edition. London, 1825

—— Geraniaceæ. 5 vols. 8vo. 1820-30

—— The British Flower Garden. 8vo. 1823-9. Second series. 1831-8

—— Hortus Britannicus, &c. London, 1826. 8vo.

—— Cistineæ. London, 1830. 8vo.

JOHN BUONAROTI PAPWORTH. Rural Residences . . . with Observations on Landscape Gardening. London, 1818. 4to.

—— Hints on Ornamental Gardening, &c. London, 1823. 4to.

1820 HENRY FIELD. Memoirs . . of the Botanic Garden, Chelsea, belonging to the Society of Apothecaries. London, 1820. 8vo.

JOHN LINDLEY. Rosarum monographia; or a botanical History of Roses. London, 1820. 8vo.

—— Instructions for collecting and planting seeds and plants in foreign countries, &c. London, 1823. 8vo.

—— Introductory lecture on Botany. London, 1829. 8vo.

—— A Synopsis of the British Flora. London, 1829. 12mo.

—— The Genera and Species of Orchidaceous Plants. London, 1830-40. 8vo.

—— An Introduction to the . . . Natural System of Botany. London, 1830. 8vo.

—— An Introduction to Botany. London, 1832. 8vo.

—— An Outline of the first principles of Horticulture. London, 1832. 8vo.

—— Ladies' Botany, &c. London, 1834. 2 vols. 8vo.

—— A Key to structural, physiological, and systematic Botany. London, 1835. 8vo.

—— Flora Medica; or Botanical Account of the more important plants used in Medicine, &c. 1838. 8vo.

—— Sertum Orchidaceum. Coloured plates. 1838. Folio

—— School Botany: an explanation of the characters of the principal . . . Flora of Europe. 1839. 8vo.

—— The Theory of Horticulture; or an attempt to explain the . . . operations of gardening upon physiological principles. London, 1840. 8vo.

—— Pomologia Britannica. London, 1841. 3 vols. 8vo.
Assisted in Vol. III. by R. Thompson.

—— Orchidaceæ Lindenianæ; or notes upon collection of orchids . . . by Mr. J. Linden. London, 1846. 8vo.

—— The Vegetable Kingdom. London, 1846. 8vo.

—— A Glossary of the technical terms used in Botany. 1848. 8vo.

—— Folia Orchidacea. London, 9 parts, 1852-59. 8vo.

—— The Symmetry of Vegetation. London, 1854. 8vo.

—— Descriptive Botany. 1858. 8vo.

RICHARD PIGOTT. A Short, plain Treatise on Carnations and Pinks. 1820. 8vo. *

CUTHBERT WILLIAM JOHNSON. An Essay on the uses of Salt for agricultural purposes. London, 1820. 8vo.

—— Observations on the employment of Salt in Agriculture and Horticulture. 1825
Several later editions—the 11th in 1835.

1821 HON. AND REV. WM. HERBERT. Appendix to the Botanical Magazine and Botanical Register. London, 1821. 8vo. *

HENRY PHILLIPS. Pomarium Britannicum, an historical and botanical account of fruits known in Britain. London, 1820. 8vo.

—— New Edition, under the title Companion to the Orchard. London, 1827. 8vo.

—— History of Cultivated Vegetables. London, 1822. 2 vols. 8vo.
This is said to be the second edition, but the date of the first edition is not known.

—— New edition under the title, Companion to the Kitchen Garden. 1831. 2 vols. 8vo.

1821 —— Sylva Florifera, or the Shrubbery Historically . . treated. London, 1823. 2 vols. 8vo.

—— Flora Domestica. London, 1823. 8vo.

—— Flora Historica; or the three Seasons of the British Parterre, etc. London, 1824. 2 vols. 8vo.

—— Floral Emblems. London, 1825. 8vo.

—— Sylvan Sketches. London, 1825. 8vo.

WILLIAM COBBET. The American Gardener; or a treatise on the situation and laying out of gardens, &c. London, 1821. 12mo.

—— The Woodlands; or a Treatise on Planting. London, 1825. 8vo.

—— The English Gardener . on the situation . . . and laying out of Kitchen Gardens, &c. London, 1829. 8vo.

SIR WILLIAM JACKSON HOOKER. Flora Scotica. London, 1821. 8vo.

—— Exotic Flora. Edinburgh, 1822-27. 4to.

—— A Catalogue of Plants in the Royal Botanic Garden, Glasgow. Glasgow, 1825. 8vo.

—— The British Flora. London, 1830. 12mo.

—— Botanical Miscellany. London, 1830-33. 3 vols. 8vo.

—— Icones Plantarum. London, 1836. 8vo.

—— Botanical Illustrations. London, 1837. 4to.

—— Flora Borealis Americana. London, 1840. 2 vols. 4to.

—— Genera Filicum. London, 1842. 8vo.

—— Niger Flora. London, 1849. 8vo.

—— Filices Exotica. 1857-59. 4to.

—— Garden Ferns. 1861. 8vo.

Outline of a General History of Gardening. London, 1821. 8vo.   *

DE CANDOLLE.—Elements of the Philosophy of Plants, translated into English from the German translation of Théorie Elementaire de la Botanique by Augustin de Candolle, with additions by K. Sprengel. Edinburgh, 1821. 8vo.

1822 Hortus Anglicanus; or Modern English Gardening. London, 1822. 2 vols. 12mo.   *

These two works, without the authors' names, are mentioned by Johnson.

F. D. LEVINGSTON. A Practical Treatise on the Growth and Culture of the Gooseberry. London, 1822. 12mo.

WILLIAM SALISBURY. The Cottagers' Agricultural Companion, &c. London, 1822. 12mo.

1823 PATRICK NEILL, M.A., F.L.S. Journal of a Horticultural Tour through some parts of Flanders, Holland, and the North of France, &c. Edinburgh, 1823. 8vo.

CHARLES HARRISON, F.H.S. A Treatise on the Culture and Management of Fruit Trees. London, 1823. 8vo.

—— Horticultural Register (with Sir Joseph Paxton). 1831-36

DONN. Catalogue of Plants. 1823

Plan for cultivating Grapes in the Field. Liverpool, 1823. 8vo.   *

    Mentioned by Johnson without the author's name.

1824 THOMAS WATKINS. The art of promoting the growth of the Cucumber and Melon, in a series of directions for the best means to be adopted in bringing them to a complete state of perfection. London, 1824. 8vo.

WILLIAM DEAN. Hortus Croomensis. Worcester, 1824. 8vo.

THE GREENHOUSE COMPANION. Anonymous. London, 1824   *

—— The second edition. London, 1825. 8vo.

1825 B. MAUND. The Botanic Garden. (Published monthly), 1825 to 1850. 4to.

RICHARD MORRIS. Essays on Landscape Gardening. London, 1825. 4to.

P. W. WATSON. Dendrologia Britannica. London, 1825. 2 vols. 8vo.

G. BLISS. The Fruit Grower's Instructor, &c. London, 1825. 8vo.

WILLIAM BILLINGTON, M.C.H.S. A series of Facts, Hints, Observations and Experiments on the different modes adopted for raising Plantations of Oak, with experimental remarks upon Fruit Trees. London, 1825. 8vo.

T. F. HUNT. Half a dozen Hints on Picturesque Domestic Architecture. London, 1825. 4to.

—— Designs for Parsonage Houses, &c. London, 1828. 4to.

1826 CHANDLER and BUCKINGHAM. Camellia Britannica. 8 plates. London, 1826. 4to.   *

1826 A Practical Essay on the culture of the Vine, and a Treatise on the Melon. By an experienced Gardener. Royston, 1826. 8vo.   *

A Catalogue of Fruit in the Horticultural Society at Chiswick. 1826

Flora Conspicua, a selection of the most ornamental . . plants for embellishing Flower Garden and Pleasure Ground, engraved . . by William Clark. London, 1826. 8vo.

WILLIAM WITHERS, JUN. A Memoir on the Planting and Rearing of Forest Trees. Holt, 1826. 8vo.

—— A Letter to Sir Walter Scott, Bart., exposing certain fundamental errors in his late Essay on the Planting of Waste Land, &c. Holt, 1828. 8vo.

1827 JAMES MITCHELL. Dendrologia; or a Treatise of Forest Trees, &c. Keighley, 1827. 8vo.

Account of the different Flower Shows in England during 1826. Ashton-under-Lyme, 1827. 12mo.   *

Account of the different Gooseberry Shows in England during 1826. Manchester, 1827. 12mo.   *

Catalogue of Fruits cultivated in the garden of the Horticultural Society of London, at Chiswick. London, 1827. 8vo.

W. COLLYNS. Ten minutes' advice to my neighbours on the use and abuse of Salt as a Manure. 1827   *
Described by Johnson as having passed through four editions.

1828 SIR HENRY STEUART OF ALLANTON, BART., LL.D., F.R.S. The Planter's Guide, &c. Edinburgh, 1828. 8vo.

SIR JAMES SINCLAIR, BART. On the Culture and Use of Potatoes. Edinburgh, 1828. 8vo.

CHARLES MACINTOSH. The Practical Gardener and Modern Horticulturalist. London, 1828. 2 vols. 8vo.

Practical Instructions for the formation and culture of the Tree Rose. Anonymous. London, 1828. 12mo. *

JOHN SAUNDERS. The Kitchen-Garden Directory, &c. London, 1828. 12mo.   *

1828 SIR WALTER SCOTT. On Ornamental Plantations and Landscape Gardening. (Quarterly Review.) 1828

JAMES GRAHAM TEMPLE. The Scotch Forcing Gardener. Edinburgh, 1828

1829 The Domestic Gardener's Manual, being an Introduction to Gardening on Philosophical Principles. By a Horticultural Chymist. 1829. 8vo.   *

JOSHUA MAJOR. A Treatise on the Insects most prevalent on Fruit Trees, &c. London, 1829. 8vo.

—— Theory and Practice of Landscape Gardening. London, 1852. 4to.

GEORGE WILLIAM JOHNSON. A History of English Gardening. Chronological, biographical, literary, and critical. 1829. 8vo.

This is the work to which frequent reference is made in the above list of books.

—— The Gardener's Almanack. London, 1843. 12mo.

—— The Principles of Practical Gardening. London, 1845. 8vo.

—— The Potato Murrain and its Remedy. London, 1846. 8vo.

—— A Dictionary of Modern Gardening. 1846. 8vo.

—— The Cottage Gardener. Conducted by Johnson. 1849, etc. 4to.

—— The Cottage Gardener's Dictionary. 1852. 12mo.

This work went through many editions and was often republished with supplements. The second edition, 1857, 8vo., has the same title as that of 1852. Later on it was called *Johnson's Gardeners' Dictionary*. The latest edition was revised by C. H. Wright and D. Dewar. London, 1894. 8vo.

—— Gardening for the Many. London [c. 1856]. 8vo.

By Johnson and others.

—— British Ferns Popularly described and illustrated by engravings. London, Winchester [printed], 1857. 8vo.

—— The Garden Manual. By the Editor and Contributors of the " Cottage Gardener." London, 1857. 8vo.

—— Science and Practice of Gardening. London, 1862. 8vo.

1829 GEORGE DON. Encyclopedia of Plants. London, 1829. 8vo.
—— A General System of Gardening and Botany, founded
   upon Miller's Gardener's Dictionary. London, 1832-8.
   4to.

1830 THE DOMESTIC GARDENER'S MANUAL . . . . to which is
   added A concise Naturalist's Kalendar, and English
   Botanist's Companion. By a Practical Horticulturist.
   London, 1830. 8vo.

1831 SIR JOSEPH PAXTON. The Horticultural Register (with
   Charles Harrison). 1831-36
   —— The Magazine of Botany. (Begun in 1834.) 16 vols.
   8vo.
   —— Practical Treatise on the culture of the Dahlia. 1838.
   12mo.
   —— Pocket Botanical Dictionary. 1840
   JOSEPH HARRISON. Floricultural Cabinet. 1833-51. 21 vols.
   8vo.

1835 JAMES MAINE. The Villa and Cottage Florist's Directory.
   1835
   JOHN DENNIS. The Landscape Gardener. Chelsea, 1835.
   8vo.
   CLEMENT HOARE. Practical Treatise on the cultivation of
   the Grape Vine on open walls. London, 1835. 8vo.

1836 R. MARNOCK. The Floricultural Magazine. 6 vols. 8vo.
   1836-41
   LOUISA ANNE TWAMLEY. The Romance of Nature, or the
   Flower Seasons illustrated. London, 1836. 8vo.

ADDENDA

1602 The Orchard and the Garden, containing certaine necessarie, secret and ordinarie Knowledges in Graffting and Gardening. Wherein are described sundry waies to graffe, and diuers proper new plots for the Garden Gathered from the Dutch and French. Also to know the time and season when it is good to sow and replant all manner of Seedes [Woodcut]. London, Printed by Adam Islip, 1602. 4to.

> The above is the title of a book in the University Library, Cambridge, and no other copy is recorded.

STEPHEN SWITZER—Since writing the note (*see* 1715), I have seen a work by him entitled,

> The Practical Kitchen Gardiner, or a New and Entire System of Directions, For his employment in the Melonry, Kitchen-garden, and Potagery, in the several Seasons of the year—being chiefly observations of a Person train'd up in the Neat-Houses or Kitchen Gardens about London . . . etc. The whole methodiz'd and Improv'd by Stephen Switzer. London, 1727. 8vo.

SIR HUGH PLAT (*see* 1594). The Garden of Eden, also reprinted 1654, 1659, 1660, and 1675

SAMUEL GILBERT (*see* 1682). Florists' Vade Mecum. One copy in B.M. is dated 1683, called 2nd edition, another 1690, one in the University Library, Cambridge, is dated 1693, and I have a copy called 3rd and enlarged edition, 1702

PETER COLLINSON (*see* 1792). Wrote for the "Phil. Trans." in 1729, not for the "Linnean Soc. Trans."

SPECIAL ADDENDA

TO THIS REPRINT

1558 ALEXIS—WARDE. The Secretes of Alexis of Piedmont containyng excellente remedies against divers diseases, woundes and other accidents. . . . Translated out of Frenche into English by Wyllyam Warde. . . . J. Kingston for N. Inglande. London, 1558. 4to. (B.M. Cat.)

—— Another edition "neuely corrected and amended and also somewhat enlarged in certaine places whiche wanted in the fyrst edition." Imprynted at London by Rowland Hall for Nicholas England, 1562. Small 4to. In three parts, with a separate pagination and Index to each

—— Other editions, 1568, 1580

1559 PETER MORWYNG. A new book of Destillation of Waters called the Treasure of Euonymous, containing the wonderful hid Secrets of Nature touching the most apt Formes to Prepare or Distill Medicines. . . . Translated (with great diligence and care) out of Latin by Peter Morwyng, Felowe of Magdaline Colledge in Oxforde, Imprinted at London by John Day. . . . There is no date on the title-page, but the preface is dated 2nd of May, 1559. Small 4to.

—— Another edition, dated first day of June, 1565. John Day, London. Small 4to.

1640 I. H. Δενδρολογια. Dodona's Grove or the Vocall Forrest, by I. H. Esquire. Printed by T. B. for H. Mosley. . . . London, 1640. 4to.

(*See* 1706) RICHARD BRADLEY. A General Treatise of Husbandry and Gardening, containing such observations and experiments as are useful for the improvement of land . . . with a variety of curious cuts, by Richard Bradley. Printed for T. Woodward . . . and J. Peele . . . London, 1724. 3 vols. 8vo.

(*See* 1713) JAMES PETIVER. Hortus Peruvianus Medicinalis, or the South-Sea Herbal. Containing the names . . . of divers medicinal plants lately discovered by Pere L. Feuille . . . London, 1715

1719 TOURNEFORT ——. The Compleat Herbal : or the Botanical Institutions of Mr. Tournefort, . . . carefully translated from the original Latin, with large Additions from Ray, Gerarde, Parkinson, and others, . . . with a short Account of the Life and Writing of the Author. London, 1719. 4to. with plates

(*See* 1724) PHILIP MILLER. Figures of the most beautiful useful and uncommon Plants described in the Gardener's Dictionary, exhibited on three hundred copper plates. . . London, 1760

—— Another edition. 1771

(*See* 1746) DAVID STEVENSON. The new and complete Gardener's Kalendar, or the Gentleman and Gardener instructed in Sowing, Planting . . Sixth edition. Dublin, 1765

(Said to be the same work as that quoted 1746.)

1748 PIERRE POMET.—A Complete History of Drugs, written in French by Monsieur Pomet. . . To which is added what is farther observable on the same subject from Messrs. Lemery and Tournefort . . done into English from the originals. 4th edition, carefully corrected with large additions. London, 1748. 4to.

—— Earlier editions. 1712-1725

1750 WILLIAM JOHN HALFPENNY. Rural Architecture in the Chinese Taste, being designs for the decoration of gardens, &c. Second edition. 4 parts, with 60 plates. London, 1750. (*See* 1755)

1754 EDWARD KNIGHT. " Dovers' Legacy, The British Legacy or Fountain of Knowledge," containing " The Gardener's Legacy," by Edward Knight. London, 1754. 8vo.

(*See* 1757) WILLIAM MASON. The English Garden, a Poem in four books

> In an edition, with a general title-page, printed by A. Warde. Yorke, 1781. 4to. On the title to the first book it is called "the third edition," London, 1778, and on that of the second book "the second edition," York, 1777. Book the third, London, 1779, and Book the fourth, York, 1781, containing "A General Postscript."

1763 WILLIAM CHAMBERS. Plans, Elevations, Sections, and Perspective Views of the Gardens and Buildings at Kew, seat of the Princess of Wales. With 43 plates. London, 1763. Roy. fol. (*See* 1772)

(*See* 1763) THOMAS MARTYN. Rousseau's Letter. 1766. 8vo. (See 1763)

1767 W. WRIGHTE. Grotesque Architecture. Consisting of plans, elevations, and sections for summer and winter hermitages, grottos, cascades, . . . &c. 29 plates. London, 1767

—— New edition. London, 1790

1773 N. WALLIS. The Carpenter's Treasure, a collection of designs for temples . . . and bridges in the Gothic taste . . . a complete system for rural decorations. New edition, with 16 plates. London, 1773

(*See* 1777) JOHN KENNEDY. A Treatise on Planting, Pruning, and on the Management of Fruit Trees, by John Kennedy, Gardener to Sir Thomas Gascoigne, Bart. London, 1777

(*See* 1787) WILLIAM CURTIS. Observations on British Grasses. London, 1790. 8vo.
—— Other editions. 1804, 1812

1796 J. PLAW. Ferme Ornée, or Rural Improvements. A series of domestic and ornamental designs suited to parks . . . &c. London, 1796

(*See* 1797) WILLIAM SALISBURY. "Hints to the Proprietors of Orchards and Growers of Fruit in General." London, 1816. 12mo.

(*See* 1803) JOHN CLAUDIUS LOUDON. The Gardener's Magazine and Register of Rural and Domestic Improvements. Conducted by J. C. Loudon. London, 1826-1834. Second series, 1835-1843. 8vo.

1807 G. Tod.   Plans, Elevations, and Sections of Hot-houses
. . . including a hot-house and green-house in Her
Majesty's Gardens at Frogmore.   London, 1807

(*See* 1809) Sydenham Edwards.   The new Botanic Garden, with
133 plants engraved.   2 vols.   London, 1812.   4to.

1824 Thomas Forster.   The Perennial Calendar and Companion
to the Almanac, with Paragraphs headed " Flora."
1824.   8vo.

—— Pocket Encyclopædia of Natural Phenomena for the
use of . . . Gardeners and Husbandmen, &c.   Containing " Flora Spectabilis."   London, 1827.   8vo.

1833 W. Cobbett.   The English Gardener, or Treatise on the
situation, laying-out, &c., of Kitchen Gardens, . . .
formation of Shrubberies and Flower Gardens, &c.
London, 1833

1837 Barton and Castle.   The British Flora Medica.   London,
1837.   2 vols. 8vo.

AUTHORS OF WORKS ON GARDENING

The dates refer to the first edition of each Author's earliest work

ABERCROMBIE, JOHN 1767
Acton, J. 1809
Adam, James . . . 1789
Addison, Joseph . . . 1712
Agricola, George Andrew . 1717
Aiton, William . . . 1789
Aiton, Wm. Townsend (1810) 1789
Amos, William . . . 1794
Anderson, James . . 1777
Andrew, Lawrens . . 1527
Andrews, Henry . . . 1797
Archer, Clement . . . 1798
Astley, Francis Duckenfield . 1797
Attiret, J. D. (*see* Beaumont) 1752
Austen, Ralph . . . 1653

BABINGTON, C. C. (Trans.
 Linn. Soc.) . . . 1791
Bacon, Sir Francis . . 1625
Banks, Sir Joseph (Hort. Soc,) 1812
Barnes, Thomas . . . 1758
Barrington, Hon. Daines . 1769
Bauer, Francis . . . 1796
Beale, John 1613
Beaumont, John (Phil. Trans.) 1665
Beaumont, Sir H. (*i.e.* Jos.
 Spence) 1752
Bickham, George . . 1750
Billingsby (*see* S. B.) . . 1669
Billington, William . . 1825
Blagrave, Samuel . . . 1669
Blair, Patrick . . . 1720
Blake, Stephen . . . 1664

Blakewell 1737
Bliss, G. 1825
Blith, Walter . . . 1649
Bobart, Jacob . . . 1648
Bolton, James . . . 1785
Boothby, Sir B. (Hort. Soc.) 1812
Borde, Andrew . . . 1540
Bowles, Rev. W. L. . . 1835
Bradley, Richard . . . 1706
Braddick, J. (Hort. Soc.) . 1812
Braunschweig (*see* Hollybush) 1561
Brocq, Rev. Philippe le . 1786
Brookshaw, George . . 1812
Browne, Robert . . . 1786
Browne, Sir Thomas . . 1658
Brulles 1790
Brunswick, Jerome of (*see*
 Andrew) 1527
Bryant, Charles . . . 1783
Bucknal, Thos. Skip Dyot . 1797
Bute, John, Earl of . . 1785

CANDOLLE, A. de . . 1821
Carey, Walter (*see* W. C.) . 1525
Carter, Daniel . . . 1767
Castel, Robert . . . 1728
Catesby, Mark . . . 1731
Carlisle, A. (Hort. Soc.) . 1812
Carpenter, Joseph . . 1717
Caux, Isaac de . . . 1645
Chambers, Sir William . 1772
Chandler (and Buckingham) 1826

Churchy, G. (*see* Dubravius)   1599
Clarke, G.   1715
Cobbet, William .   .   .   1825
Colebrooke, H. T. (Trans.
Linn. Soc.)   .   .   .   1791
Coles, William   .   .   .   1656
Collins, Samuel   .   .   .   1717
Collinson, Peter (Trans. Linn.
Soc.)   1791
Collyns, W.   .   .   .   1827
Commelin (*see* G. V. N.)   .   1683
Commerell, Abbé de (*see* Lett-
som)   1774
Cooke, Moses   .   .   .   1676
Copeland, W. (*see* W. C.)   .   1525
Cotton, Charles   .   .   .   1675
Cowell, John   .   .   .   1729
Cowley, Abraham   .   .   1667
Coventry, Francis   .   .   1753
Cullum, Sir Dudley   .   .   1694
Culpepper, Nicolas   .   .   1652
Cunningham, James (Phil.
Trans.)   1665
Curtis, S. (*see* J. Maddock) .   1822
Curtis, William   .   .   .   1787
Cushing, John   .   .   .   1814

D ALTON, JOHN .   .   1755
Darwin, Erasmus   .   .   1791
Dean, William   .   .   .   1824
Dede, James   .   .   .   1809
Dennis, John   .   .   .   1835
Dethick (*see* Thomas Hill) .   1563
Dicks, John   .   .   .   1771
Dickson, James   .   .   .   1785
Dickson, R. W.   .   .   .   1804
Dillywn, L. W. (Trans. Linn.
Soc.)   1791
Dodoens, Rembrant (*see* Lyte)   1578
Don, George   .   .   .   1829
Donn   1823
Donn, James   .   .   .   1796
Donovan, E. O.   .   .   .   1790
Dove, John   1770
Drope, Francis   .   .   .   1672

Dubravius, Janus (*see* trans-
lation)   1599
Ducarel, Andrew Coltee   .   1773
Ducket, Thomas .   .   .   1659
Dunbar, John (Hort. Soc.) .   1812

E DWARDS, SYDENHAM   1809
Ehret, Geo. Dionysius .   .   1767
Ellis, John   1770
Ellis, Thomas   .   .   .   1779
Ellis, William   .   .   .   1685
Ellis, William   .   .   .   1732
Elsholt (or Elsholtz, John
Sigismond, *see* Sherley) .   1677
Emmerton, Isaac .   .   .   1816
Estienne, Charles (*see* Surflet)   1600
Evelyn, Charles .   .   .   1707
Evelyn, John   .   .   .   1658

F AIRCHILD, THOMAS .   1722
Fairweather, J. (Hort. Soc.) .   1812
Falconer, William   .   .   1783
Farmer, J.   1735
Felton, Samuel   .   .   .   1785
Field, Henry   .   .   .   1820
Fitzherbert, Sir Anthony   .   1523
Fleetwood, Wm. (Bishop of Ely) 1707
Forster, John   .   .   .   1664
Forster, John Reinhold .   .   1771
Forsyth, William   .   .   1791
Forsyth, William (the younger) 1794
Frampton, John .   .   .   1577
Freeman, Strickland   .   .   1797
Fulmer, Samuel .   .   .   1781
Fuller (Hort. Soc.)   .   .   1812
Furber, Robert   .   .   .   1727

G ANDON, JAMES .   .   1715
Gardiner, Rev. James .   .   1718
Gardiner, Richard   .   .   1599
Garton, James   .   .   .   1769
Gendre, Le Sieur Le (*see*
Forster)   1664
Gentil, François Le (*see*
London and Wise) .   .   1699

Lawrence, Anthony (*see* Beale) 1536
Lawrence, John . . . 1714
Lawson, William . . 1618
Le Blond (*see* James) . . 1703
Lee, James 1760
Lettsom, John Coakley . 1774
Levingston, F. D. . . 1822
Liebault, John (*see* Surflet) . 1600
Liger, Louis (*see* London and
 Wise) 1699
Lightoler, T. . . . 1762
Lille, l'Abbé J. de (*see* also
 Montolieu, 1800) . . 1783
Linacre, Thomas . . . 1530
Lindegaard, Peter . . 1811
Lindley, George . . . 1796
Lindley, John . . . 1820
Linnæus (*see* Forsyth, Jen-
 kinson, and Milne)
Lister, Martin (Phil. Trans.) 1665
Lisle, Edward . . . 1757
Lobel, or L'Obel, Matthias de 1570
Locke, John . . . 1766
Loddiges, Conrad . . 1777
Loddiges, G. (Hort. Soc.) . 1812
London, George . . . 1699
Loudon, Mrs. (*see* Loudon) . 1803
Loudon, John Claudius . 1803
Lovell, Robert . . . 1659
Lunan, John . . . 1814
Lunwenhock, Anthony van
 (Phil. Trans.) . . . 1665
Luttrel (Hort. Soc.) . . 1812
Lyon, Peter . . . 1813
Lyte, Henry . . . 1578

Marnock, R. . . . 1836
Marshall, Rev. Charles . 1796
Marshall, William . . 1785
Martyn, Thomas . . 1763
Mascall, Leonard . . 1572
Mason, George . . . 1768
Mason, W. Wallis . . 1806
Mason, William . . . 1757
Matthews, H. S. (Hort. Soc.) 1812
Maund, B. . . . 1825
Maunsell, William . . 1794
Mawe, Thos. (*see* Abercrombie) 1767
Maxwell, Robert . . 1757
McPhail, James . . . 1794
Meader, James . . . 1771
Meager, Leonard . . 1670
Mean, James . . . 1817
Merret, Christopher (Phil.
 Trans.) 1665
Millar (or Miller), Joseph . 1722
Miller, John . . . 1779
Miller, Philip . . . 1724
Mills, John . . . 1759
Milne, Rev. Colin . . 1770
Mitchell, James . . . 1827
Monardes, Doctor Nicholas
 (*see* Frampton) . . 1577
Montolieu, Mrs. . . . 1805
Morgan, W. (Hort. Soc.) . 1812
Moriarty, Mrs. Henrietta M. 1806
Morison, Robert . . . 1672
Morris, Richard . . . 1825
Mortimer, John . . . 1707
Mountain, Dydymus (*see* Hill) 1563
Murray, Lady Charlotte . 1799

MACDONALD, ALEX. . 1807
Macer (*see* Linacre) . . 1530
MacIntosh, Charles . . 1828
Maddock, James . . 1792
Maher, J. (Hort. Soc.) . 1812
Maine, James . . . 1835
Major, Joshua . . . 1829
Malthus 1783
Markham, Gervaise . . 1613

NEALE, ADAM . . 1779
Neill, Patrick . . . 1823
Newton, James . . . 1752
N. F. . . . 1604 and 1608
Nichol, Walter . . . 1797
Noehden, G. H. (Hort. Soc.) 1812
North, Francis Dudley (Lord) 1669
North, Richard . . . 1759
Nourse, Timothy . . 1700

Stevenson, Rev. Henry . 1716
Stillingfleet, Benj. . . 1759
Surflet, Richard . . . 1600
Sweet, Robert . . . 1818
Swinden, N. . . . 1778
Switzer, Stephen . . 1715

TAVERNER, JOHN . 1601
Taylor, Adam . . . 1769
Taylor, Joseph . . . 1812
Temple, James Graham . 1828
Temple, John (Phil. Trans.) 1665
Temple, Sir William . . 1685
Thompson, James . . 1757
Thornton, Robert John . 1799
Todd, George . . . 1812
Townsend, A. . . . 1726
Tradescant, John . . 1656
Trowell, Samuel . . . 1739
Trusler, John . . . 1780
Turner, J. (Hort. Soc.) . 1812
Turner, William . . . 1538
Turton, William . . . 1802
Tusser, Thomas . . . 1557
Twamley, Louisa Anne . 1836

VAN OOSTEN . . 1703
Venables, Rev. J. (Hort. Soc.) 1812
Vispre, Francis Xavier . 1786

WALPOLE, HORACE . 1770
Ward, Rev. Samuel . . 1775
Warre, J. (Hort. Soc.) . 1812

Watkins, Thomas . . 1824
Watson, P. W. . . . 1825
Watson, Sir William . . 1748
Watson, William . . . 1807
Webb, W. 1753
Wedgewood, John (Hort. Soc.) 1812
Weeks, E. 1814
Weston, Richard . . . 1769
Wheatley (or Whately), Thos. 1770
Wheeler, James . . . 1763
Whitmill, Benjamin . . 1763
Williams, J. (Hort. Soc.) . 1812
Wilbraham, R. (Hort. Soc.) . 1812
Wildman, Thomas . . 1768
Wilkinson, T. (Hort. Soc.) . 1812
Wilmot, John Eardley . 1815
Wilson, Alexander . . 1780
Wilson, John . . . 1744
Wilson, William . . . 1777
Winter, George . . . 1787
Wise, Henry . . . 1699
Withering, William . . 1776
Withers, William, jun. . 1828
Wolfe, C. J. . . . 1715
Woods, T. (Trans. Linn. Soc.) 1791
Woodville, W. . . . 1790
Wooton, Sir Henry . . 1624
Worlidge, John . . . 1669
W. S. 1609
Wyer, Robert (*see* Macer) . 1530

YONGE, EZEKIEL (Phil.
  Trans.) 1665

Authors mentioned for the first time in the Special Addenda.

Alexis (*see* Warde) . . 1558
Barton 1837
Castle 1837
Cobbett, W. . . . 1833
Forster, Thomas . . 1824
I. H. 1640
Knight, Edward . . 1754
Morwyng, Peter . . 1559

Plaw, J. 1796
Pomet, Pierre . . . 1748
Tod, G. 1807
Tournefort 1719
Wallis, N. 1773
Warde, William . . . 1558
Wrighte, W. . . . 1767

www.ingramcontent.com/pod-product-compliance
Lightning Source LLC
Chambersburg PA
CBHW030026030726
47499CB00008B/3133